Jamaican Sunrise

The Complete Series

A BWWM BILLIONAIRE ROMANCE

Jaelynn McCranie

Publisher's Note: This is a work of fiction. Names,
characters, places and incidents are a product of
the author's imagination. Locales and public
names are sometimes used for atmospheric
purposes. Any resemblance to actual people, living
or dead, or to businesses, companies, events,
institutions, or locales is completely coincidental.

Jamaican Sunrise/ Jaelynn McCranie -- 1st ed.
Xplicit Press, an imprint of TLM Media LLC

ISBN-13: 978-1-62327-654-6
ISBN-10: 1-62327-654-3
eISBN 978-1-62327-655-3

Printed in the United States of America

CONTENTS

1

"Let me see..." Alex says, not really looking at the menu. He is sitting in a beachfront eatery off the coast of Jamaica after his meeting ended sooner than planned, and he is enjoying the view. Yes, the beach is beautiful, Jamaica always is. His waitress, though, has caught his attention, more so than the menu even.

"Would you like more time sir," she says, after a while, Sabrina very pleasant, and generally very patient. She has been looking at the businessman, white, 40ish, she thinks, in his unbuttoned shirt so crisp that you can tell that just minutes earlier, it had a tie wrapped neatly around the collar.

Alex has also been watching Sabrina, her skin the most beautiful shade of ebony, hardly older than 25. He knows that he probably doesn't stand a chance with her, but that is alright; he tells himself. He thinks briefly of his life so far, two failed marriages and a son he never sees, who is probably around the same age as this woman he cannot help but steal another glance at. Alex does not know where to turn his gaze when she is suddenly walking towards him.

He hides his head in the paper, not really reading the front page, but needing to appear as though he is. Sabrina reads the back of the paper, for just a moment, before she asks him if he is ready to order. He lowers the paper, and for the first time in a long time, he has nothing to say. He has not even looked at the menu, he realizes, and so he doesn't even know what is on offer. He knows what he would like to say, but still, he restrains himself.

"The Asian economy is gaining real traction…" is all he manages, after glancing at the front-page headline briefly. He realizes immediately that he could have done a little better than that, but it is too late now.

"Off the back of extreme human capital reserves, and policies that are mostly unfavorable to the poor...but I suppose that is the price of progress, or regress, depending on whether or not you're of the communist persuasion..." she responds, realizing too that she probably ventured too much of an opinion. She thinks quickly how to recover from this, hoping to at least secure the standard fifteen percent tip from her serious businessman looking client. "Can I recommend the Cajun chicken?"

He agrees to the recommendation without thinking, taken completely by surprise with her opinions on the Asian economy. When she walks away, he immediately starts to think of how he can further press, just to see if her response to this world phenomenon was not just a fluke or a rehearsed response, prepared to keep the business clientele engaged to just ensure that they leave her with a generous gratuity.

When she brings him his meal, he is armed with an artillery of questions, but he paces himself. He leads her down a path that touches on almost every major story in recent times, from the antics of Boko Haram to the mining industry in South Africa. She has an opinion on all of them, and this is not just a general opinion either. She is well read, and up-to-date with the goings on in the world, and this makes for a refreshing change from the standard meaningless banter that one has come to expect from a waitress.

By the time he has finished his meal, he is more than a little intrigued by the twenty-five-year-old Jamaican beauty, who has introduced herself simply as Sabrina. He thinks that he managed to say his name, but he cannot be sure; his thoughts consumed with how incredibly intelligent and out of place, this beauty is in this restaurant. He would imagine that she should be the PA to a media executive somewhere, with her finger on the pulse of world affairs.

He looks at her fingers as she removes his plate from in front of him, and for a split second, he imagines the same fingers working their way on parts of his anatomy that he really should not be thinking of right now. Sabrina has captured him, however, in a very short space of time. She is that rare combination of brains and beauty, and he wants to own her immediately, to nurture her and see the young flower blossom into everything that she can be, given the right opportunity.

Alex pays his bill and leaves her with a tip twice the size of the cost of his meal. He thanks her for her incredible service, and admires her for her remarkable grasp of world affairs. On a whim, he writes his phone number on the back of the bill and encourages her to call him if she ever found herself in the States. He has no idea if she will call him, though, and as he leaves the restaurant, he wishes that he was leaving with her, just to talk to her, to see how deep her soul goes, and how far her knowledge actually stretches.

He thinks of Sabrina on the flight home, and even as he unlocks his New York penthouse, she is running through his mind. He wonders if she would have given him her number if he had asked. As he passes the hallway mirror on his way to his master bedroom, he stops in front of it and takes off his shirt. He has aged well, he thinks. Alex also resolves to make more time to get to the gym, because he is bulging slightly in places that he would rather not be.

In the shower, his mind is again on Sabrina. He wonders about her life in Jamaica, and invents an entire backstory for her. He knows that the facts of this story are probably mostly incorrect, but for the purposes of imagination, and his ego, he needs her to be a helpless damsel in distress, just waiting for the right knight to come riding along to rescue her from her plight. He makes up his mind to be that knight.

The following Sunday, Alex cannot take it anymore. He has given it a week, thinking that if he did not shake the urge to see her again, he would make a day trip to Jamaica. He catches the earliest flight out of New York and arrives on the island paradise shortly after 10 AM. He hopes that Sabrina is working, and he hopes that the restaurant is open for breakfast. Alex arrives at the beachfront restaurant just after 11 and is disappointed to find that Sabrina is not working.

"Will Sabrina be in today," he eventually asks the manager.

"Yes, she is working the lunch shift, she should be here any moment now; can I get you a drink while you wait for her..." The manager seems to have something to say to Alex, to ask him, but he manages to hold himself back, going to get the tropical punch that Alex has ordered.

Alex watches the entrance of the restaurant, nervous excitement developing rather quickly in his stomach. What is he going to say to her? He is not even sure why he has come here, but he just knows that he really has to see her again. He rehearses a conversation in his head, and then scraps it. He rehearses another conversation and then realizes that he cannot be fully prepared for any conversation with the young woman, not knowing how she will respond to any of the questions that he has given her answers to in his head.

Sabrina arrives to work, but he does not see her. She uses the staff entrance in the back, goes through the kitchen, and goes straight to the back room where the staff gets changed. After changing into her uniform, and pulling her hair into a high bun and out of her face, she grabs her order book and pen from her backpack and stuff them in the front pocket of her apron. She walks out into the main restaurant, folding her cloth, and greeting everybody that she meets.

Alex spots her in his periphery and almost chokes on the sip of tropical punch that is already in his mouth. He recovers, though, and takes another sip, just to clear his throat. He watches her talk briefly with the manager, who must be telling her about him because both of them are looking his way. He watches her adjust her skirt, and then apron, and watches her pull an imaginary strand of curly black hair out of her face, as she walks towards him. Every conversation he has rehearsed in his mind is now gone.

She is standing in front of him too soon, and he is looking in her eyes, with no words coming out of his mouth. He knows that he should probably say something soon, or risk coming across as a creepy older man who has just one thing on his mind. He looks away from her for a second, gathers himself, and then looks back up at her again.

"Hello, Sabrina..." He is not sure how she will read the fact that he has remembered her name.

"Hello, Alex..." She remembers his name too, which evens out the playing field.

Silence again hangs between them, but it is not uncomfortable. Alex just looks at Sabrina, with a smile forming on his face, a smile that he cannot help. She cannot help but returning the smile, although she keeps on turning her face away, searching her mind for something that she could say. Nothing comes to mind, and this worries her because she is looking around the filling restaurant, at the tables that she is missing. She starts to think of an exit strategy, but still, Alex has not said what he has come here to say.

Sabrina does not look at Alex that way, not at all. Alex is, however, looking at her in many different ways, wondering which one is the best way to use to break the ice. He doesn't know if he should just offer her a job, a position that he is prepared to create for her, in New York, or if he should just ask her out on a date. Sabrina's next words give him the direction he needs to know which approach is best, however.

"Is there anything that I missed the last time we spoke? Did China suddenly reform their employment policies, or has India put a definitive framework in place with regards to child labor that I should know about?" Sabrina smiles as she asks the questions, not expecting Alex to take them seriously at all.

"Well, that is exactly why I'm here... However, I think this conversation will be better had in New York City, with you doing a short internship at one of my companies..." Alex says it, not sure how it sounds to her, but knowing what it would sound like to him if the roles were reversed.

"New York, huh..." Sabrina processes this request, knowing somehow that Alex is serious. She needs time to think about this but knows that he is expecting an answer. She remembers something her grandmother used to always say to her, that when the opportunity to change your life presents itself, you should not question it...you should embrace it. She shakes the thinking demons from her head and takes a deep breath. "When would this internship start?"

"Tomorrow..." Alex says, not wanting to waste any more time.

That is how Sabrina found herself packed and ready to leave Jamaica. This Sunday night would mark the beginning of the rest of her life. Alex arranges for her flight the next morning and books her hotel accommodation for two weeks. He will work out the details of her internship Monday morning, and set her up in New York quickly, wanting to make her as comfortable as he can, as he puts in place his plans to woo her.

In less than a month, Sabrina is set up in New York City. She has a small one-bedroom apartment overlooking Central Park, fully furnished of course, with a fridge full of food. She has a job with Ramsey Media, as assistant to Alex's personal assistant, who is a young gay man named Lyle, about her age, so he really doesn't mind the help. He has to ask, though, where Alex found Sabrina, and when, in her naivety, she relates the story to him, he is immediately intrigued, wanting to be her new BFF.

Lyle makes Sabrina his personal project, and in the month, she looks every bit like a New Yorker, without losing any of her Jamaican, island girl style. Alex has held himself back from pursuing Sabrina too, mostly because he has been busy, but also because he does not know if she would be interested in him that way. She has however noticed traits in Alex that she finds remarkably attractive, and except for the fact that he is a middle-aged white man, he would be her perfect match. She too, however, has hidden her interest very well.

At the end of the first month, however, Alex has his first Saturday free, and so he decides that it is now or never. He consults with Lyle, who is more excited than he is at this possibility. Lyle too has an older boyfriend, and he has always thought that Alex would be quite a catch. Even if it is a heterosexual, cross-cultural liaison, he supports it wholeheartedly, even though some of Alex's friends are less than impressed with the new addition to his staff. They have their suspicions, but Alex is not saying anything. The men think he's developed a mid-life taste for the exotic, and the women in his circle resolve to keep an eye on the little *gold-digger.*

Alex is not concerned about his friends, though, always dancing to the tune of his own drum. He does not even know if Sabrina would be interested in him, so he cannot give their concerns and comments much mind. After Lyle arranges the intimate dinner at a café near Sabrina's apartment, Alex has to pluck up the courage to ask her out. The hours seem to move swiftly by on the Friday afternoon too so that he knows that he is running out of time if he is to make full use of his free Saturday.

"Sabrina, come in..." he says after he has Lyle send her to his office.

"Yes, sir?" She says, wondering if she has perhaps done something wrong already.

"Feel free to say no...But I'm free tomorrow evening, and I was wondering if you would like to join me for dinner...," he says finally, after another long, comfortable silence, and the exchange of smiles that has become a regular thing between them.

"Yes, sir...sure" Sabrina says, not sure what to make of this, but remembering again her grandmother's advice.

"Alex, please...call me Alex!" he says, breathing a subdued sigh of relief.

For the next month, the two of them eat out regularly. Sometimes they have lunch, sometimes dinner. Sometimes lunch becomes dinner, the pair never running out of things to say to one another. Alex learns Sabrina's true backstory, how she was raised by her grandmother, how she has six brothers, how she was saving up to go to a local nursing college. She learns how he made his fortune, how it all started with a small student film, and then to the production of training materials for businesses all over the world. They discuss each other's likes and dislikes, their favorite things, and everything in between.

It takes them one month to feel like they have known each other for a million years. It takes them one month to feel closer to one another than they have ever felt to anybody else in their entire lives. It takes them one month for them to fall absolutely in love with each other, and for them to feel that the time has come for them to take their relationship to the next level. They both have apprehensions, though, for different reasons, so when Sabrina says to Alex *'do you want to come up'* after a late dinner, he almost says no.

Alex has a problem, and this has nothing to do with his vasectomy. Although, he does secretly hope that Sabrina also does not want any children, but if she does, she is the one woman that he would reverse it for. Alex's problem is a physical one, though, and it is a rather large one. He packs quite a lot of meat between his legs, and judging from Sabrina's tiny frame; she might not be able to take him. He has had sex, with many women, and he knows that he is an uncomfortably large penis. It is too late for him to turn back now, though, as Sabrina unlocks the front door to her apartment and lets him in.

She pours them both a glass of wine, a bottle that she was keeping for just this moment, whenever it happened, and she puts on a pot of coffee, to round it off. She knows that if they get to the coffee, then tonight will not be the night, and she isn't sure if she will be disappointed if it isn't. She is very nervous now, and this must show because Alex pulls her close to him, and after planting the first kiss on her lips, long, sensuous, and passionate, he says the words that make her relax a little bit more.

"We don't have to do anything that you are not ready for Sabrina, you know that right?" he whispers in a husky whisper, letting her know that he really wants her.

"I know... but I really want to..." Sabrina says, not knowing the full length and girth of the challenge that lies ahead.

They put down their glasses, and Alex asks her to show him the bedroom. He is also nervous now, not sure how she will respond to his penis when he finally whips it out in all its exaggerated glory. His erection has started to form already, and the bulge in his pants is a dead giveaway. He resolves to keep her eyes from his crotch, kissing her again, looking at her closed eyes, hoping that her hand does not go down to meet his mammoth python, and she goes running for the hills, literally.

Alex turns her so that she is facing away from him now, and he unzips her dress. He lets it fall to the floor, and she steps out of it and turns back to face him. They are kissing again, and her nipples are hard, brushing up against his chest, still covered with a shirt. He is a little self-conscious about the little bit of a stomach that he has developed over the years and makes a mental note to start hitting the gym with earnest. There is nowhere for him to hide his stomach now, though, as she starts to unbutton his shirt, and work it off his arms.

He works on her bra, and as it drops to the floor, he follows it, and is on his knees, sniffing around her crotch area. This is a lucky escape for him because she was already working on his belt. He will get his own pants off, but first he will distract her with his mouth on her cunt. It works too, and as soon as he has removed her panties, she drops her pussy into his mouth, and he undoes his own belt, pants button, and zip. His pants go as far as his knees, which are on the floor as he works his tongue over the surface of her pussy.

Alex brings himself to his feet again and walks her over to the bed, his pants around his ankles now. He turns her away from him again, and works his shoes off, and then his trousers. He manages to get his underwear off as well before she turns around to look at him, and by the time she does, he quickly turns her back again, so that her back is to him, and he takes off his socks. They are both naked now, and he considers turning her back to face him. Instead, though, he pushes her onto the bed so that she is lying on her stomach.

He turns her over so that she is on her back, and he goes for her pussy immediately with his mouth again. Alex kisses her pussy all over the surface of it and then nibbles gently on her clit. It is quite engorged now and pushes through the soft covering of black curls blanketing the cunt. Her pussy is neatly trimmed, but it is not clean shaven, and Alex finds this very hot. He doesn't know when was the last time he had the pleasure of encountering an unshaven cunt, which is one of his undeniable fetishes.

Sabrina does not know whether to hold onto his head or to touch her breasts. Both of these actions are rather tempting, but she does not want to take anything away from Alex, who seems determined to give her maximum pleasure. She decides to go for his head, and hold it slightly in place, leaving her breasts open for Alex to touch, whenever he is ready. She does hope, though, that it is going to be very soon, her hardened nipples needing some serious attention, quickly.

Alex suddenly reaches for her tits, landing on them with his first attempt. He keeps his mouth on her cunt, and as he gives both her breasts a firm squeeze he enters her slit with his tongue. He fucks her with the tip of his tongue for the longest time, while he presses down on her mounds, which are perched so perfectly on her chest that he could not miss them if he tried. He sends more of his tongue into her cunt and is pleased to find it quickly becoming incredibly wet. Sabrina has not been fucked for a while, and Alex too has had no sex since he first met Sabrina, so they are both extremely needy.

He reaches into her pussy with all of his tongue now, and she is not sure if he is suddenly possessed of a cock in his mouth. It is thick and hot, and wet and nothing like the delicate organ that he was using in her mouth earlier. She gasps, literally gasps, placing her hands on his head to make sure that he was still fucking her with his mouth. He is incredibly attentive to every detail of her pussy, and he pays the most intimate attention to all of these details, all of these parts of her that have been largely ignored by previous lovers.

His hands work on her breasts too, with the same attentiveness, and he pinches her nipples between his fingers so that she squirms. Sabrina wraps her legs around his head now, as she gets closer and closer to orgasm. She knows that she will not be able to hold herself back from cumming any longer, even if she tries, never having such an expert tongue-lashing on her pussy before in her entire life.

When she blows, Alex's tongue is still inside her, and it absorbs into it like a sponge. He laps up the liquid that is pouring through the walls of her cunt, like open floodgates, and he is enjoying every drop of it. He never expected her to be a huge *squirter*, but she is, and he is pleased, for reasons known only to himself for the moment. He will have to introduce her to his *not so little friend* soon, though, and he can only hope that she is wet enough to receive him. If not, then, at least, he will have the satisfaction of knowing that he brought her to at least one epic orgasm, and he can eat out her pussy all night if that is all she can manage, he tries to convince himself.

2

When Alex comes up to kiss Sabrina on her mouth again; his dick rubs up against her thigh, and Sabrina catches her breath. She is not sure if what she is feeling is really what she thinks it is, so she has to be sure. She raises her leg between Alex's legs and makes contact with his balls. The sack is large, too large, and his balls fall on either side of her knee. Sabrina needs to be sure of what it is she felt initially, so she searches for his dick again.

When she makes contact with the tool again, she loses her breath completely. Sabrina had never looked at his crotch before, never curious as to what lay inside his pants. She has been focused on getting to know the man, and now, she wishes that she would have had a little bit of warning about what to expect, knowing of course that it is too late for her to turn back now. She will have to see this through, and she can only hope that she can take the massive dick into her tiny pussy. Sabrina knows that this is going to be quite a challenge, though.

Every time his dick makes contact with her pussy, she freezes, however. This is completely involuntary, and she wishes that Alex would just ram his cock inside her so that she can make peace with this invasion. Alex knows, however that this is quite a task, and he will not force Sabrina to do anything that makes her uncomfortable. His meat throbs now, though, wanting to be inside her, having waited very long for this privilege and pleasure.

She tries to open her legs, to let him know that he can take her, but her legs try to cross over each other. Sabrina wants to see what she is getting herself in for, but there is no way for her to look down between her legs, Alex's chest tucked into hers tightly. She returns her focus to his lips now, wrapping her legs around his, willing him to take her. She really hopes that he takes her quickly, now that her pussy is still wet, and able to receive him.

Alex places his dick at the entrance to Sabrina's pussy, and he rubs the tip of his mammoth dick against her clit and then works some of his pre-cum on her slit. She releases some more moisture from deep within her pussy, as much out of fear and apprehension as desire. Sabrina really wants Alex, all of him, and so she braces herself for his entry, knowing that it won't be too long now. She senses, from the way he is kissing her that he too really wants to be inside her now.

He nudges gently into the space between her cunt-lips, and then he positions his missile for launch. Alex opens his eyes now, watching her face, her eyes closed still, and he starts to press against her entrance now, hoping that her pussy will give way. It doesn't, resisting even the one inch that he is trying to get inside her. He presses on, though, kissing her deeper, sending his tongue into her mouth, hoping that her pussy will start to receive him too.

When she eventually lets a few inches' slip into her, he is relieved, but still holding back, not wanting to invade her too quickly. Still, he appreciates the progress that he has made, and he fucks her gently with the few inches that are already inside her. She parts her legs a little more, wanting him to go as deep as she can take it, but realizing what he is doing. She too has an incredible appreciation for this, knowing that he is aware of his problem, and that he knows just what to do about it.

When she starts to feel the beginnings of an orgasm, she realizes what she needs to do. As she starts to flow with the product of her climax, she lifts her ass off the bed, feeding her cunt to Alex swiftly, so that two-thirds of his dick is lodged inside her pussy. Again she is breathless, but she is also incredibly relieved that she has taken him into her, as far as he is probably going to go tonight. She starts to grind her cunt against his cock, and Alex starts to thrust into her gently, feeding her just these two-thirds or so of his thick meat.

Soon enough, he is progressing steadily towards his own orgasm, not as complete as he would have liked, but not expecting any more from the tiny Sabrina. He exercises incredible restraint and drives the parts of his dick that are inside her in an out, in and almost all the way out. He needs to create distance between the beginning of the thrust and its end so that he can cum with a little sense of satisfaction. Alex is grateful for her, though, and he really appreciates the parts of her that she has let him have.

When he finally cums, she too has another massive orgasm. They cum together, two more inches of his dick slipping inside her. He parks it in her warmth and exhales into her mouth. Then he kisses her gently before rolling onto his back, bringing her with him so that she now straddles him. She is nervous; knowing that in this position there is nothing to stop the full length of his shaft from disappearing inside her. Alex knows this, though, and he holds her up above her waist. She relaxes into his grip, knowing somehow that he will not let her go, and thereby drop her onto his waiting cock, which seems primed to impale her.

He moves her back and forth on the parts of him inside her hot pussy. Sabrina forgets quickly the precarious position she is in, and she concentrates on the cock inside her now. Alex is stronger than you would think looking at him, and he holds her quite firmly above himself. She grinds against his dick now, making him almost lose his grip, though, but she seems oblivious to this. Soon enough, they are both having another orgasm, and then he eases her down so that she can reach his lips. Part of him still remains inside her, though, and as his cock softens and hardens he keeps thrusting gently into her.

When they lie side by side, his cock is still in its location, fattening and thinning slightly, but no longer invading her. She has relaxed totally into the tool now, her pussy muscles completely relaxed. They talk for the longest time, Alex hinting that he might be ready to go again, not once making any indication that he wants to leave. So, after making love for the last time, he pulls Sabrina close to him, and he watches her fall asleep in his arms. He is a very happy man, falling asleep shortly after.

There are a million things that go through Sabrina's mind come morning. She has no time to think of them, though because Alex is still there. After a quick shower, and breakfast, he finally leaves, not wanting to, but having a 7:30 conference call. It's Sunday, but by now Sabrina knows how he works. She likes to watch him in action too, so commanding and in control of everything. He pays as much attention to the details of his business as he did to her body last night. She cannot believe what an incredibly attentive, gentle lover he was. Already she is having fantasies about the next time.

She tells herself that it will be easier the next time, now that she knows what to expect. Sabrina had not imagined that Alex's cock would be as big as it was; she had not even thought about it. She places a hand on her pussy, congratulating it for its incredible achievement. She can only hope that it will not be too long before he is inside her again, knowing that if you wait too long between sexual encounters, every time can feel like your first. It certainly is nothing like riding a bike.

Come Monday, it seems like everyone knows what went down on Saturday. Everyone except Lyle looks at her with renewed contempt, and she does not know why. She knows that the men are not homosexual and that the women were not dating Alex, so why the resentment, she wonders. Thinking about it, though, she sort of understands where they are coming from. She was just a waitress on an island saving up for nursing school, and now she is the assistant to the PA of a middle-aged media magnate. She doesn't like the associations she herself is making with this story.

"Will you come to the club with me on Saturday morning," Alex asks her after a midweek tryst. He really seems unable to get enough of her.

"The club..." Sabrina asks, knowing immediately that this will draw so much attention to them, and everyone will start talking; really start talking.

"Yes Sabrina, the club... I know that you have reservations about being seen with me, but I think it's time to let society know once and for all that we're dating...we are dating, right?" He teases her with this question while threatening her pussy with another invasion from his bazooka.

"It isn't you...really it isn't. It's just that, people have been talking..." She stops herself immediately, realizing that if she focused on what people said, she would not do anything in her life. She also knows that at Alex's age, he definitely is not bothered with the opinions of other people. "Oh fuck it, yes, I'll go with you... of course I will!"

"Good..." he says and shows her his appreciation with another round of beautiful lovemaking.

Saturday comes too quickly for Sabrina's constitution. She feels like she is going to throw up, almost like she is a lamb being led to the slaughter. As she gets dressed, she looks at herself in the mirror, knowing that any wrong move now will just feed her detractors perceptions of her and her relationship. She settles for a Chanel pants suit; a gift from Alex, to give her an air of sophistication that she knows is not there. Nobody needs to know this, though, and all her dresses just seem too short for the New York Country Club, and the last thing she needs is to come across as a hooker or a mindless bimbo.

They walk into the club just after 11, just in time for the brunch traffic to start. This is strategic from Alex's viewpoint, wanting to jump in at the deep end, to get it over and done with quick and fast. He walks her into the reception area and plants a kiss on her mouth as they are being shown into the main dining area. He kisses her a few more times as they are shown to a VIP table, that is clearly visible from all exits and entrances into the space, and from almost every table. After Sabrina sits, Alex gives her one more kiss for good measure, and then he sits down, picking up the menu, and perusing it casually. Sabrina feels the stares like icy daggers on her back. Alex doesn't give a fuck.

Alex has also received words of caution from various corners. He hasn't paid this much mind, though, hoping that when his friends see how serious he is about Sabrina, that they will back off. He lets it go, for the moment, and returns his energies to

Sabrina, who is looking a little more comfortable, a little more relaxed. The crowd soon fades into the background, and Alex doesn't even notice the people who are not coming to say hello to him. He just enjoys Sabrina's company, and they have a beautiful brunch that becomes lunch, and then afternoon cocktails. When he is sure that his point has been made, he gives Sabrina one last kiss, and then they make their way out if the club, much to Sabrina's relief.

Over the next couple of weeks the pair field comments and questions from all and sundry. Sabrina often feels overwhelmed, but Alex takes it all in his stride. He has enough years behind him to know how to navigate negative commentary, Sabrina not so much. He tries as best he can to protect her from this onslaught too, but he cannot be with her at all times, so he just has to trust her ability to handle herself. He knows that she has a good head on her shoulders and that she will not let the detractors get her down.

Another problem is looming, however, peeking over the horizon like a thief peeping over your wall, casing your house, planning to rob you of your most prized possessions. He has noticed how some of his friends have started to look at Sabrina, with keen interest, and lust. He thought he was imagining it initially, middle-aged insecurities, but he knows in his gut, in that place that knows, that it is more than that. They want her, to take her from him, to feel what he feels when he is with her, to taste what he tastes. Alex knows that they are not even interested in anything else, and for them it would just be about sex. How can he protect Sabrina from this temptation?

Will she be tempted, though, he asks himself? If so, then she is certainly not the principled young woman that he has fallen for. He doubts this, though, but he still needs to be sure. He decides just to watch her reactions to this attention that his friends are showing her, knowing that he will know, either way if she is really the woman for him. Alex hopes that Sabrina passes this test, and although he feels bad for even putting her in this position, he really just needs to know.

He needs to be 100% sure that she is committed to him, and only him, and that she will not give in to the first offer that appears more attractive.

"Are you happy?" he asks, about three months into their relationship. This question is unexpected, so it takes Sabrina a while to respond.

"Of course I am; why would you ask me that?" She thinks she knows, though. Even if he doesn't show it, his friends' behavior is getting to him.

"You would let me know if there is anything that makes you unhappy, won't you?" He seems unable to ask her what is really on his mind.

"Alex, I am happy... and while your friends make me a little uncomfortable, there is nothing outside of this, right here, which will result in a breakup. So no, you have nothing to worry about. There is nothing that anybody can do to make me not want to be with you. Only you can do that!" She answers all his questions.

"I will never give you a reason to doubt my love for you..."

"And I will never give you a reason to doubt me..."

They both sound very sure of what

they are saying to each other. They are very sure. Love has blossomed very quickly for the two of them, and neither of them expected this. Now that it is here, though, in all its glory, they both embrace it. They are fully prepared for the challenges that lie ahead for their kind of love. The road ahead will not be easy. They know this. Together, though, they will weather whatever storm comes their way, and they will always find their way back to one another.

Seeing each other becomes more and more intense with the passing months. They see each other every day now, and even when Alex is out of the country, Sabrina flies out to him if he will be there longer than the time it would take her to reach him. Nothing about this liaison is wrong, not for them, and they grow closer with each encounter. They quickly become inseparable, and after five months, they are unquestionably, undoubtedly, and irrevocably in love.

Sabrina has gone from a shy, self-conscious woman into a confident vixen in this time. She has indeed gone through the most amazing metamorphosis, and Alex loves the change. He loves that he has been a part of this growth, viewing Sabrina as his special little project, one that he has intense feelings for, and one who returns these feelings. He knew from the moment he met her that she was special, but he had no idea how special. Now that he knows, he is certain that losing her will really affect him badly.

Still, his friends are becoming a real problem now. They do not even seem to notice when he is around, making a pass at Sabrina at every opportunity. He ignores it for the most part, not because he does not want to deck them, but because he wants to see Sabrina's reaction. He just needs to be sure, once and for all, of her feelings for him, because this relationship has developed very quickly. This is just one hurdle that he hopes they can overcome, and then he will have no problem taking their relationship to the next level.

Thoughts of marriage are actually starting to consume him now, even though Sabrina has not let him know in any way that she is ready for this step. He thinks that it is ridiculous that he is even thinking of marriage so quickly, but he does. He cannot hide it, and he certainly cannot deny it. He thinks of every possible strategy to eliminate this risk, but he knows that the only way to overcome this is to go through it. There will either be love at the end of this challenge, or the end of what was promising to be a beautiful future, for Alex at least. Alex tries to contain his anxiety and to give this situation one more month before he asks Sabrina to be his wife.

He decides to get them away for a weekend. He can manage three days, so he decides to take them to the Cayman Islands. He has a house there, and he is yet to show it to her. Alex knows that Sabrina is not impressed by wealth, but he has nothing but his money and himself to give to her. Small gifts have never been his strong point, and even a three-day trip has got to be luxurious. That is just how Alex Ramsey rolls and the woman in his life has got to just deal with it. Sabrina has managed quite well with the elevated status of the venues that they have eaten at so far, and she looks perfectly at home in her apartment. She has also adjusted quite well into his penthouse a beautiful mix of old and new, dripping in extravagant minimalism.

They leave on Thursday evening, using a small plane that Alex shares with his friends. It is really his plane, but he doesn't use it as often as he knows he should. Alex has always preferred to travel commercially, enjoying the interaction with other people. Yes, he always travels business class, but he enjoys talking business with fellow moguls, enjoying these conversations simply because they get his mind off his own business. He very seldom has the opportunity not to think about his own business.

They arrive on the Cayman's just after 8 PM, and the even is beautiful. There is a breeze on the island, a calming breeze that seems to hug you and caress you. Alex wants to block Sabrina's eyes as they approach the house, knowing that it is an incredibly beautiful home, but he holds himself back, thinking that this will be too much of a cliché, that he will come across as conceited, almost, and so he just watches her face as they approach the sprawling cliff-side mansion. He sees all the questions forming on her face, but none of them are articulated out of her mouth.

She is star struck, and she can almost not contain herself. She keeps herself in check, though, keeping the questions to herself. One of the most prominent questions on her mind though is why he would have such a huge house on an island that he doesn't really visit. He explains this, though, without her having to ask, and she takes his answer for what it is. He also does not know why he feels the need to explain this, probably just to break the silence.

"I know it's large, and it is a bit much... but my friends and I usually use it together, a couple of times a year. Although mostly it's them, they pretty much have free reign of the place..." Alex stops himself, feeling like he is mumbling.

"I see..." is all Sabrina says in response, shocked by the full complement of staff on hand to meet them on their arrival at the front door. She looks at Alex, reprimanding him for this excess. She knows though that he probably has more money than he knows what to do with, so he just spends it in pockets, creating jobs for as many people as he can, regardless of where in the world they are.

Alex greets everybody, and every single one of his staff members is very excited to have the master of the house here. They greet Sabrina as enthusiastically, but they are cautious with her, it seems. She knows why. It is probably the fact that Alex has brought other women to this house, so they do not want to become too attached to her, not yet. They have probably seen many lovers come and go.

He notices this, and he watches how she handles it. She has so much style and grace; it is incredible to watch. Alex wants to take her and kiss her right there and then, but he has never been one who shows public affection easily. He really wants to, with Sabrina though, foregoing every rule that he has ever had about relationships. He thinks of taking her on a tour of the house, but then he thinks better of it. It will look better in the morning, and besides, dinner is waiting for them already in the dining room.

They sit down to eat while two maids take their bags up to the master suite. It is actually more a master wing, private in every sense of the word. You would be forgiven for thinking that you were in a different house altogether. The suite takes the most advantage of every possible view from the house, and so it is really the best place to be in the morning. Alex knows this, and he cannot wait to see her face in the morning. Dinner first, though, and they walk through to the elaborate dining room.

The couple sits close to each other at the end of the table. They chat while course after course comes out of the kitchen in front of them. There is a moment's pause with every course that is placed before them, and then they are back to talking with each other, touching each other's faces, and stealing kisses. When dinner is finally over, they take a glass of wine each on the terrace and take in the sea breeze. Now they kiss passionately, and while the staff cleans up inside and then disappears. They seem to know that their services will not be required anymore tonight.

3

When they make their way to the master bedroom, Sabrina catches her breath, again. There are so many little pockets in this house, on the way to the room, that seems to call you to explore them. There is no time for that, though, Alex wanting to get his woman alone, behind closed doors, under lock and key, so that they can explore each other. The large windows that are actually doors are open in the room, and the curtains are open too so that the same breeze that was caressing them downstairs moments earlier dances all over the exposed parts of their bodies.

Alex cups Sabrina's face, his thick fingers touching her cheeks gently. She likes the feeling of his fingers on her, and she leans into this touch, letting all the stress of working and life back in New York fade away. Some moments slip into this night that threatens to take it away from them, however, moments where Sabrina thinks of all the names she has been called, moments where Alex questions some of the warnings that his friends have been throwing his way. Then he looks down at Sabrina, and she looks up at him, and all these things become irrelevant.

He takes off her dress in one move, and then her bra. Then he pulls her panties down and takes a whiff out of her cunt. This sends immediate blood flow to his cock, which is rock hard in his pants now. He has been dancing between hard and semi-hard all night, trickles of precum escaping his massive dome. At last, now it seems that he is about to have clear access to her runway, and he has every intention of parking his Boeing on it tonight. Patience is one of Alex's great virtues, though, and so he is in no rush.

The size of his dick probably has something to do with the patience that he has developed over time. This patience doesn't translate to his work, though, but it doesn't have to. Work is work, and play is play. There are little opportunities for impatience when he plays, especially not if he wants full on penetration. This is all he wants with Sabrina. He wants to feel all of her, on all of him, for as long as she can possibly take it.

He licks her pussy, nibbling on her clit, urging it to produce its tell-tale moisture. He doesn't have to wait too long either, because soon she is dripping out between her lips, and he is lapping it up. The taste and smell of her turn him on incredibly. She is incredibly aroused by the cross between hot and cold on his tongue. She steadies herself by placing her hands on his head. This frees his hands up to remove his dick from the restraint of his pants. He is so focused on the work his tongue is doing that he doesn't even realize that he has managed to undress himself completely.

Sabrina comes down to join him on the soft rug. There is no need for him to hide himself anymore since she knows the full length and girth of his dick. She knows it very well indeed. Alex is still on his knees, with his hands in Sabrina's hair now, as she attempts to take his meat in her mouth. She succeeds too, tasting the sensual sweetness of his precum. Her tongue makes quick work of this liquid, and then she goes down a quarter of his shaft, hiding it between her lips. Her teeth make direct contact with the flesh on his dick, unavoidable for obvious reasons.

She manages to get half of his dick in her mouth now, and then works back up to his head. Her tongue runs circles around this mushroom, and just to where the remainder of his circumcision gathers right under it. Again she envelopes the top of his meat with her mouth, and again she ambitiously goes for a little more than half of it. Again she succeeds, but not for long. She recovers to the head again, just so that her jaw can relax a little bit.

Alex lifts her off him now, knowing

that for all her enthusiasm, he is just too thick for her to make any real inroads on his dick, at least not with her mouth. He lays her down on the rug and watches her body respond to the breeze coming into the room. It has actually become a real gust of wind, but it is not cold, so it is comfortable. Her nipples are hard, and her breasts are perkier than they usually are, something that Alex didn't even think was possible. He takes one of them into his mouth and sucks on it, rather aggressively.

When he moves over to the other one, she cannot help but reach down for her pussy. She touches her clit lightly, and then sends two of her fingers into herself. She reaches for his rod too and strokes it with the same rhythm that she is dishing out on herself. Her hand does a better job on his dick then her mouth did, strangely, and soon enough he feels like he could cum at any moment. He throws his eyes down to where she is working on herself, and he likes what he sees.

He watches her work on herself, all the while keeping his mouth on her breasts. He doesn't even look at her hand on his own tool, not needing to, feeling every one of her fingers as they move up and down the full length of his shaft. When she starts to have an orgasm he has to stop sucking on her tits and watching her fingers move swiftly in and out of herself, he comes up on his knees, like he is standing over a meal that he is about to devour.

Alex takes in the sight before him, and as she starts to come down from her orgasm, he lifts her up off the ground and carries her to the bed. After putting her down on it, he goes to turn off the lights and makes a mental note to have the lighting redone in the house so that it can be turned off at the clap of your hands, or, at least, a switch closer to the bed. He gets to the bed, mounts it, and finds her lips quickly. She kisses him back as passionately, reminding him why he loves her.

Then he turns Sabrina on her side and faces her ass towards his cock. He will not dare try for this space, not yet, it is way too soon. He runs his fingers down the side of her, from her ribcage, over her hips, then onto her thigh, appreciating the pear shape. She really is beautiful from every angle. Alex kisses her back, down to the ball and then up to the back of her neck, slow and deliberate. She arches her back into his lips and then relaxes into the kisses raining down on her. Her eyes are closed, and he loves that she now trusts herself completely with him.

He lifts her leg and rests it on his, tucking himself underneath her almost. He looks down to where his cock is already grazing her pussy, and he likes the view. Alex now has a full view of himself, and he will be able to watch himself disappearing inside her tight pussy when she is ready for him that is. He rubs the head of his cock against her clit, and against the entrance to her pussy. She couldn't close her legs now if she tried, her one leg hanging on Alex's, keeping it firmly in place.

He holds her in place and sends just an inch of his massive python into her. She takes a deep breath and holds it. Then he taps on her clit lightly, and she exhales. He keeps on tapping on her clit, sending the vibration of a thousand drums into her, through her cunt, up her vaginal walls, and into her belly. Alex taps a little bit harder with just two fingers, sending another inch into her, and then another. When he has succeeded in entering her with half of his thickness, he stops tapping on her clit and starts rubbing it gently.

Small circles, deep circles, and then he resumes his tapping, feeding more of his snake into her. He watches his vanilla dipstick disappearing into her ebony mound, and the vision makes his cock thicker, harder. He is careful, very careful about how he enters her. She appreciates this care, and she cannot even move her cunt on his meat now, not in the position that they are lying in. The tapping on her pussy becomes rubbing again, and he feeds more of himself into her still. He gets as deep as he is going to go, and he stops.

Then he pulls half of his advantage out of her, and thrusts it back into her, rubbing her clit the whole time. Half out, then back in, half out, and then back in as far as he will go. Alex loves the feeling of her clit on his fingertips, and he remains perched on it, rubbing it nonstop now. Sabrina's eyes are still closed, but Alex is kissing the side of her face as close to her mouth as he can get in this position. Alex cannot close his eyes, though; he is enjoying the view too much.

He watches himself move easier and easier inside her pussy, and he watches her lubrication coating his meat more and more. Alex cannot help himself but try for one or two more inches, and when he succeeds, he hits her g-spot, and she groans loudly. He stops to check if she isn't in any pain, but notices the smile on her face, her eyes are still closed, and he knows that he has hit the elusive spot. He hits it again and again, and then he pauses right on top of it, and he presses it down firmly with the head of his cock.

Sabrina is cumming again, wetting herself from the inside, and wetting Alex's meat too. This lubrication allows him to slip one more inch into her, but that is all that he is going to get. Three-quarters of his dick now sit safely inside her, and he loves the quarter or so that he sees peeping out of her pussy. This is a truly beautiful sight, and he thrusts in and out of her with these three-quarters until he too finally comes to his climax. He is so steady, so controlled, something that he has perfected over time.

Losing this hold that he has on her now is not an option. He has gone deeper than ever before, knowing that he has filled her the way no man has filled her before. He eases her onto her stomach, and rolls on top of her, his dick still firmly in place. He loses his erection but regains it rather quickly. The gym is really serving him very well. In five short months, he has toned up incredibly, and his dick is more of a power ranger than it ever was before.

He places his hands underneath her chest and takes a firm hold of her breasts. He squeezes gently on them, thrusting into her as gently, resurrecting his hard-on. When he is at full mast again he starts to go at it with real verve; gentle verve mind you, but verve nonetheless. He parts her legs a little more with his own legs, bending his knees, and pulling her with his dick into himself a little more. Then he is digging deep into her, threatening her with yet another orgasm. She submits to these threats, and soon enough she is creaming again.

Alex kisses the side of her face, and

then the back of her neck and the top of her back. He really wants to turn her over, but he is not yet ready to remove himself from her. He has an idea, but if it is going to work, she will need to use all the strength left in her. He gives her a moment to gather herself, and another moment just to make sure that she has some of her strength back. Then he turns onto his back, taking her with him. He brings her up to sitting, her back to him, and he holds her up at the waist.

Then, slowly, very slowly, he starts to pivot her on his cock. His meat is stiff again, a raging hard-on that threatens to impale her if he lets go of her waist. But they have been in this position before, and she trusts him. She holds herself up with her hands, and lifts her ass, so that her pussy is not on his meat completely, half of him inside her now. She needs to do this, to make allowances for any sudden slips. Eventually, after the longest time, she is facing him, and she slowly stretches her legs out towards the back of her, so that his legs envelope hers now, her chest on his now, her nipples sinking into the hair there.

She kisses him now, hard, she almost wants to swallow him into herself. He feels the same way, holding her face against his, determined to taste every part of her. They enjoy each other, sucking on one another's tongues with an intensity mirrored only by the love they have for one another. Theirs has really been a whirlwind romance, everything happening so quick, so fast, that they haven't had any time to process it all. One thing they are sure of, though, both of them, is that they are incredibly in love with each other.

He starts to pump again, filling her up with his sausage so that she feels him almost in her heart. She is usually very uncomfortable in this position, hoping that it will be over soon. But love has taken over completely now, and she is willing to take him anyway, anyhow, now. She is willing to sacrifice herself totally for his satisfaction, and he knows it. He likes that she is willing to give herself to him, and he knows that he can make her happy, in every possible way.

And he does too. He fills her up to overflowing and then milks her, along with himself, until she is panting again. She has never had so many orgasms in such quick succession, everyone feeling different, everyone with its own unique flavor. She knew somehow that the patience would eventually pay off, and that she would eventually become accustomed to Alex's size. Now he seems to fit her perfectly, and she cannot imagine being fucked by another man. All her past lovers have been totally forgotten.

Sabrina had never thought that sex was important. She had always seen it as just an addendum to relationships. Now, though, with Alex, it is as important as the first time he said he loves her, as important as the first kiss, as important as the first single red rose he left on her pillow, no note, just his smell left behind him while he went on to conquer the world. She has never been so holistically into someone before and never ever has she loved every aspect of a man so completely.

Alex brings them to another final incredible orgasm, and then he slips himself out of her slowly. He places his meat on her pussy, so that her clit touches his shaft, and brings her slowly down from cloud nine. He breathes into her mouth, hugging her close to him, making her feel like she is fused with him. They have nothing left to say to each other, nothing that seems necessary or important in the moment. All they need is to just be here together and to love each other, unspoken, only with feelings. It is the best possible feeling.

They wake up to the sun caressing their bodies, still fused together, still one unit. They seem to be in absolute sync with one another, knowing that they can overcome anything that is thrown their way. They are prepared for anything, although they are still not sure of how this will manifest itself. There is just something sinister in the air, whenever they are surrounded by people. All these people are from Alex's camp too, Sabrina having left everybody that she knows back in Jamaica. She does miss the familiarity, though, and sometimes this pain hits her flat in the stomach.

When Sabrina is given the grand tour of the house after breakfast, she cannot hide how impressed she is. She doesn't even feel like she needs to anymore, wanting to be completely real with Alex. There is no time for secrets between them, or for words left unspoken. Theirs is a relationship that has morphed very quickly from initial apprehension to mutual respect, to a deep and intense love. If only they could live in isolation, away from all their naysayers, then things would be absolutely perfect. But this is not a perfect world, and soon enough, they have to leave the Cayman's and go back to face reality.

They arrive back in New York late on Monday afternoon, and Alex is suddenly inundated with phone calls. He has to respond to them and respond to his emails. There is one urgent email that he ignores for the most part, but it seems to creep up into his head so that he has no choice but to open it. He gets it open and sees what he tried to avoid. It is from Fred, and it is an invitation for him and Sabrina to join them on their yacht party this weekend. Alex really doesn't want to, and he knows that Sabrina will not want to either. They know though that they really don't have a choice, Fred being one of Alex's oldest friends.

The week goes by fast, too fast, and Sabrina struggles with what she should wear. She wants to look nice for Alex, but she also doesn't want to look too nice, at the risk of tempting any of his friends who have made it very clear to her, more than once, that they want to get under her dress. She thinks of wearing a pants suit, but she knows that she will not be comfortable. And since the situation itself is not going to be a comfortable one, she decides that she will wear a dress anyway.

On Friday, she goes shopping for a dress. At Alex's insistence, she takes his credit card. She has never used his money before, not without him present, and not without him to approve the purchase, so she is very nervous. Her nerves translate to sweaty palms, and she thinks that she might be arrested for stealing the credit card. Lyle is with her, though, and he has a way of turning even the most uncomfortable situations into a big fat joke.

They settle on a dusty pink, knee length cocktail dress, something different to what they know that everybody will be wearing. Sabrina knows that she is going to have most of the eyes on her at the party anyway, and she decides that if they are going to look, she might as well give them something to look at. She will wear silver and black stilettos and carry a pink and silver clutch. She is ready, well as ready as she is going to be for tomorrow's party, and so she goes home to get a good night's sleep. She does go for one drink with Lyle though, to thank him for everything.

In her apartment she thinks of what Alex might wear. She wants to dress appropriately, wants him to dress appropriately so that they look every bit like a couple. She hopes that this will get the message across loud and clear and that they will start to leave them alone. She has the idea though that this will not be possible, and she doesn't really care. She is concerned however about what Alex will think of his friends when he finds out what they have been up to.

She meets Alex in the front of her building, and she is happy with how he is dressed. He is wearing khaki pants a white shirt, making him look very relaxed. Next to Alex, she looks sophisticated and as relaxed, making them look like a super-chilled couple. She gets into the car, and they make their way to the yacht club near the Hamptons, and the drive is long. They appreciate that the drive isn't a quick one because it gives them a moment to relax and get into the mood. Although, what mood it is, they are not sure.

They arrive at the marina and walk down towards the boat, shortly after 1 PM. It is a little early, too early for them because they would have liked to arrive a little later when everyone was a bit drunk. That way they could have put all their snide comments off to the alcohol, and dismiss them soon after. Now, though, they know that everyone is sober, and they mean every single word that they say. And boy do they have a lot to say.

"So, still sinking it in the black I see..." Greg is the first to comment on Alex's relationship. His comment is uncalled for, and he is blatant about it. Alex isn't even sure if he is actually racist, or if he just has a problem with his friend sleeping with a black woman. Although, what the difference is, escapes Alex.

"Hello, Greg... her name is Sabrina. But you should know that by now, it's been almost six months..." Alex looks around for Sabrina, finding her in a conversation with Lyle's boyfriend, so he knows she is safe.

"Wow, six months...that's a little long for a casual fling isn't it?" Greg is insistent, and a real jackass.

"There is nothing casual about what we're doing. Get that into your head, my friend, before you and I aren't friends anymore..." Alex speaks firmly, and then he walks away from Greg before he says something that he will regret. Actually, he won't regret it, but he thinks that if he says anything that is really on his mind, Greg might not recover from the statements.

Alex joins Sabrina, and greets Lyle's partner, even though his name escapes him momentarily. He looks around for Lyle now and sees him near the champagne bar, struggling to fit more than two glasses in his hand. He leaves Sabrina in the safety of Lyle's partner, and goes and helps his PA, Lyle. He thinks of asking Lyle to remind him of his partner's name, but this is not necessary, the name dropping into his head suddenly, like a cherry out of the sky.

They start a casual conversation about everything but business, and they move through the crowd easily. There are some things that should really be kept for office hours, and since Danny, Lyle's partner, is not in media, they don't want to bore him with shoptalk. He is an attorney, a partner at a major Law Firm in the city, and so they keep the conversation on general matters, like the stock market and art. Sabrina, fortunately, has an opinion on everything that they choose to discuss.

Alex looks at Sabrina, and then he looks around at everybody looking at them for different reasons. He wonders if she has any intention of telling him that his friends have been coming on to her, but he doesn't even care, not really. As long as she does not respond to their advances in an inappropriate manner, then everybody will be fine. After all, if nobody moves, then nobody will get hurt.

4

"So Sabrina, you and Alex seem to be getting along rather well. You must be very grateful that he pulled you from your dreary island existence?" Mrs. Sanders speaks as though she wants everybody to hear what she has to say. Actually, she is the ex-Mrs. Sanders, her husband, having left her a few months earlier for a bohemian artist type, and they are currently backpacking through Ireland.

"Hardly... I try to get back to the island as much as possible, when Alex doesn't have me all tied up!" she responds, really having sharpened her claws over the last couple of months. She doesn't even look up to the source of these comments, focusing on the canapés in front of her, trying to choose ones that Alex might like. She knows that the innuendos in her statement are obvious, but she really doesn't care. If this is her life now, if she is really going to be with Alex, then she is going to learn to take these comments on the chin. She knows that these comments will come quick and fast too, so she has to just be ready for them when they make their ugly appearance.

She walks up to Alex with a plate and holds it out in front of him. He kisses her first, and then he points one out with his eyes. Sabrina takes the canapé in her hand and puts it in his mouth. He kisses her again before he even swallows, letting her share the half-chewed canapé in his mouth. She wipes the side of his mouth first, and then the side of her mouth. Looking around, she notices that the only other black people here are staff, and Sabrina doesn't even care about this now. She is grateful that Alex gave her an opportunity to break free from her former life. Everybody makes their bed, and everybody has to lie in it.

Then she hands the plate to Alex, and she hands him her glass. She excuses herself, needing to go to the powder room, and needing to pee. He lets her go, and he watches her walk over the deck and disappearing down the stairs. She walks down the hall and enters the bathroom as two women walk out. They look at her, up and down, surprised apparently that she is here, among them, with one of the most eligible bachelors on the boat. Their resentment is like daggers that drop coldly from their eyes.

Sabrina looks at herself in the mirror, and she pulls the skin around her eyes so that they slant. Then she lets them go, and she appreciates the firmness of her skin. She is obviously younger than most of the women here, and she certainly looks the youngest. She cups her breasts in her hands and lifts them a little higher, making them look unnatural on her chest. When she leaves them, they fall to their natural position on her front, and she realizes that she has to accept that they are perfect.

After she goes to the bathroom and finishes touching up her makeup, she opens the door. She is so wrapped up in her own thoughts that she doesn't even notice that Fred is standing in the doorway. He blocks the exit, almost as though he had been waiting for her for a while. The truth is, he has. He looks down her neck and onto her breasts. He looks down at his own crotch and takes his penis in his fingers. It shapes out perfectly, thanks to his erection.

She looks at it for a moment, making the comparison unwillingly, but she is rather smug when she notices that it is a far cry from Alex's whopper. She moves her eyes quickly off his dick and to his eyes, frowning, questioning his intentions without opening her mouth. He runs his fingers along the full length of himself now, trying to draw her attention again. She will not budge, though, not looking down once.

"Can I help you?" she asks him, not smiling, her eyes cold and hard. She has really had enough of this nonsense, and she hates the fact that these men have no respect for Alex. She doesn't mind the lack of respect for her, she doesn't even care. But she would really just appreciate it if they showed her man the respect he deserves.

"The question is, can I help you?" he asks her, trying to put a hint of mischief in his voice that wasn't there before.

"There is nothing that you can do for me...thank you anyway...now if you will please excuse me..." she says, looking past him into the hallway, wanting to be away from him.

"Are you sure?" Fred asks her, removing his erection from its perch. She cannot help but look down again, seeing the large, uncircumcised meat in his hands now. She cannot believe how blatant he is about this. He pushes her back into the bathroom and shuts the door with his back. He reaches behind himself and locks the door. Sabrina is really nervous now, and she isn't sure what the best approach will be for her to take. Screaming would draw attention to her unnecessarily.

"Fred, this will never happen..." she tries to sound as stern as she can, given the awkwardness of this situation.

"Never?" Fred asks, pulling his foreskin down over his head.

"Never...now if you don't move, this might be very embarrassing for both of us. Although I suspect a screaming woman in a locked with you exposed might be a little more embarrassing for you!" She is really anxious now, and she really wants to get out of this bathroom. The bathroom is tiny too, so tiny that if she moved an inch towards Fred, she would come into direct contact with his hardness.

Fred moves his fingers up and down his dick a little while longer, and then he moves out of the way. He watches her unlock the door and struggle a little to get out of the bathroom. He closes the door behind her and locks it again. He takes his pants off down to his knees, unable to resist this opportunity to take matters into his own hands. He looks in the cabinet for any sort of lubrication, finding hand cream. It will just have to do. He checks the door again, suddenly very paranoid. He pours some cream into his palm, and then wraps his cock in his palm, moving up and down it slowly.

He moves up and down the length of his shaft with a little more urgency, firming his grip. He gets to the head, and he rubs a little more of the cream over his now exposed head. Then he pulls down harder on his meat, and faster. He closes his eyes, and he lets them wander to thoughts of Sabrina. He imagines what her thighs must look like, and her blackberry, letting this thought consume him completely. Soon enough he is shooting his load into the sink, and he exhales hard.

After cleaning himself up, he runs some water over his cock and over his palm. Then he dries himself up and replaces his cock inside his pants. He exits the bathroom and goes to find Sabrina and Alex deliberately. He seems to enjoy taunting Sabrina, and he appears to have made it his duty to make her life difficult. Sabrina wonders how he might react if she was to tell Alex about this little agenda that he is pushing. She thinks better of it, though, not wanting to come between friends, especially not for a relationship that is just a few months old.

Alex and Sabrina are locked in conversation with each other. They don't even notice the other people that are circling them, chatting to them with ease. These people seem to be aware of the connection that the couple shares, so they don't even let it get to them. Fred tries to pass hints and insinuations for a moment, but when he realizes that he is not getting anywhere, he moves on. He turns back to look at Sabrina though, a promise that this is far from over in his eyes. Sabrina just wants to be gone from here; she wants to be off this boat and away from these people who have made it evident that they will not accept her or her relationship, not for a while.

Her man reads her like a book. He works the deck of the boat for a little while longer, and then he pulls Sabrina to him. Then he whispers the words in her ear that she has been dying to hear since the arrived. "Let's get outta here..." he whispers. She kisses him right on the lips, thanking him without having to say a word. He kisses her back, and then they make their way off the boat, saying goodbye to the people who care enough to bid them farewell. They both really couldn't be bothered by who greets them and who doesn't.

"Do you want to get something to eat?" Alex asks Sabrina as the get closer to her apartment.

"Well, I do want to eat...but food isn't top of my list..." she says to him, surprising even herself by how forward this sounds. She has just been so anxious all day that she just wants to be alone with her man, reminding him and herself that he is the only man for her.

"Really? I'm sure we can arrange something in that case...to feed your little *appetite*!" Alex is also surprised, but he appreciates that she is also starting to show some initiative. He had started to think that maybe he was forcing himself on her, making her do things that she wasn't really comfortable doing. Now he knows that she also wants him. And he also wants her, very, very much. He picks up speed now, wanting to get to the apartment quicker, to unwrap his delicate Jamaican flower.

They walk into the apartment already kissing. He is hungry for her, and she is just as hungry for him. She knows that she is in for a challenge, but she is up for it. Sabrina has started to acclimatize to Alex's size, and she knows that it will only get better with time. She knows too that he is attentive, and that he is aware of this challenge, so she gives herself to him easily. She doesn't think that she would have been able to do this with another man. Alex really cares about her, about how she feels, and about what she thinks. This is very important to her. She can overcome anything as long as he remains the attentive, caring man that he is.

She lets him undress her, and then she undresses him. He is, at last, comfortable with letting her do this, knowing that she knows just what to expect. When she gets to his boxers, she takes his dick in her hand and gives it a firm squeeze. He smiles at her, as she goes down to her knees. She pulls the shorts down past his knees and then down to his ankles. He steps out of them and stands naked in front of her.

Sabrina takes Alex into her hands, and she kisses the tip of his cock. He looks down at her, appreciating the fact that she is willing to take on this task. He watches as her mouth opens, and the first part of him disappears into her mouth. Her lips look like glistening candy wrappers as the move up his shaft and over his head. Then she is kissing the head again, just before she starts licking it like a snow cone. When she is swallowing him again, he watches each and every inch that she manages to get into her mouth.

She manages to stuff just over half of him into her mouth. She is enjoying it too, almost as much as he is. She moves from sucking to licking to biting to nibbling. He cannot tear his eyes off of her at all now, and she knows this, her eyes meeting his often. Then she closes her eyes every time she lodges him deep in her throat, keeping him there for a moment, drawing an intense moan from him. Then she works her mouth up his shaft again and focuses on his head.

This seems to go on forever, and he is certainly not complaining. Neither is she, although her jaw is starting to take strain. She is determined though to milk him at least once with her mouth. She gets close too, making more and more progress towards bringing him to an orgasm. She knows this too, and she keeps going, keeps on working on his meat until he starts to groan loudly. He feels like he is going to lose his footing, so he plants his feet firmer into her rug. Then he starts to shoot into her mouth, and he watches her response to this.

She brought this on herself, though, and he knows this. She did not expect him to shoot such a massive load into her mouth, though, and she is a little bit shocked. She gathers herself quickly, though, and she manages to swallow every drop. Not a single drop strays from his head to her mouth, and she is very proud of herself. She licks her lips, and then she kisses his cock again, affectionately. Then she licks his tip again, making sure that not s single drop of his warm lava hits the rug.

Then she takes his balls into her mouth, managing just one of the massive orbs into her mouth. She moves on to the other one, and she sucks hard on it. He is so impressed with her that he wants to lift her off the floor and thank her. She is so consumed with what she is doing, though, that he lets her continue. Then she licks his balls, and he starts to shudder. He moves back slowly, with her following him until he gets to the sofa. Then he is sitting down, and he pats her head gently while she continues to work her tongue all over his balls.

"Thank you..." he whispers.

"It is an absolute pleasure..." she whispers, and she returns to sucking on the rounds hanging just underneath his dick. His cock is still hard, and she is happy for this. She is thrilled in fact that she has this effect on him. She works her tongue from his balls up his shaft, over his head, back down his shaft, and settles on his balls again. He wants to touch her too, but it is impossible in the current position that she is in.

She brings him to another orgasm, and he cannot believe this. Neither can she in fact so that a little of his second load slips down the side of his shaft. She licks it up, though, and he gives her a look that says *well done*. After this orgasm, she comes up to standing, and then she walks over to the kitchen. She pulls a bottle of champagne from the fridge and pours them both a glass. She knows that he probably needs a break, and she needs to rinse her mouth out. She takes a huge swig of the bubbles and then places her mouth on his. He kisses her with a little more enthusiasm than usual.

Sabrina sits on his lap and enjoys his fingers moving up and down her. She opens her legs, and he makes contact with her cunt. He eases a finger inside her, and then she lies across his lap, giving him more room to work. He appreciates this, and he starts to play on her like a piano. Then he kisses her clit, and follows quickly by sucking on her pussy, and then driving his tongue into her.

She feels the beginnings of an orgasm rather quickly. There is no need for her to hold herself back, and she just lets herself go to that place where she cannot hold herself back anymore. She starts to cream, and he sucks out all the juices flowing steadily out of her. Then he drives his tongue into her again, and he is happy that she gives way easily. He licks her out with extraordinary care and impeccable attention to detail. He runs his tongue inside her, and around her on the outside of her pussy, and then again he is reaching deep inside her with his tongue.

Then he is busy with his fingers on her again. He digs into her with two fingers, and then three. Then he is fucking her with four fingers, and he does not even try to hold himself back. He pulls her cunt apart carefully, and then he puts his fingers inside her, and he pulls another orgasm from her. She closes her eyes, and then allows herself to move from this beautiful orgasm back down to earth, feeling like she is literally floating on the clouds. He is an expert at what he is doing, and he seems to be determined to bring her to a third orgasm.

Alex manages too, and he brings her to a third climax, which leaves her shaking. He bends over her and takes her up in his arms. Then he just holds her, hugging her gently. He kisses her intensely, and she starts to feel the earth again. He looks at her again, his eyes meeting her eyes, and then she is drawn into his gaze. She kisses him herself now, and he kisses her back, and then he lifts her up off the couch and carries her to the bed.

He proceeds to make the most beautiful love to her. She takes him into her as much as she can, but still not all of him. It is impossible for her to take all of him, never. She has to make peace with the fact that she will not ever be able to take every last inch of Alex into her. There is just not enough space in her for this expedition. Alex too has made peace with this fact, knowing that it will be a miracle if he were to suddenly manage to insert all of himself into her.

They lie in each other's arms afterward, sipping on champagne and chatting easily. It is amazing how easily they talk to each other, and how comfortable the silences are. Sabrina even falls asleep in his arms from time to time, and she is not even worried when she opens her eyes to catch him watching her. This relationship really feels like it has gone on for the longest time, as though they have known each other for all of their lives. This is an incredible feeling for both of them, and it is really a feeling that neither of them has felt before.

Alex watches Sabrina has she slips into sleep again. He thinks about how lucky he is, and how quickly this relationship has developed. He remembers the first day he saw her, and what he said to her. He thinks of what the circumstances have been, that have led them to this moment, and all the challenges that they have faced. He thinks about the challenges that lie ahead, and he resolves to face each and every one of them. There is nothing that can come between them, not now, not ever.

Sabrina watches Alex too when she wakes up to find him sleeping. She thinks of all the times that she has been faced with taunts and victimization at the hands of his friends, and all the times that she should have just told him about it. Then she thinks of the fact that they have hardly known each other for six months, and his friendships go back decades. She will not be the reason that he loses his old time friends, not when she isn't even sure what this is going to end up as. She has started to allow herself to think of the possibility of forever with him, though.

This forever is beautiful. She lets herself imagine what it will be like to wake up every morning with Alex's arms around her. She lets herself dream of what it will be like when his friends finally accept her and their relationship, and when they are happy for them. She lets herself go to that place in her mind where she tells her family about Alex, and they are all really very happy for her. This world seems like it is a million miles away, though, far from this current dynamic.

They both have their eyes open at the same time now. Alex kisses her forehead, and then her nose. Then he finds her lips and drinks a long drink from this fountain of love. Then he kisses her neck and finds her breasts. Then he finds the space between her thighs with his lips, feeling the need to bring her pleasure, and also to give himself some time to recover. His erection comes and goes, but it is not hard enough for him to take her again, not yet anyway. He brings her to another orgasm, and she almost loses her mind.

Then she returns the favor, and he actually manages to have an orgasm without having a full erection. This is possible at last, and he feels like a whole new chapter has been open in his lovemaking book. His body continues to surprise her, and they take each other's lips again. They fall asleep in each other's arms, fully and finally. There is no other place on earth that either of them wants to be right now. Forever is a long time, and yet they cannot imagine all of forever without each other.

Come morning Alex gets up first. He watches her sleeping for a while longer before he goes to order breakfast. There is an hour before the food arrives, and there is just a single bottle of champagne left in the fridge. Alex decides that all his work can wait, and he is going to spend every minute of this Sunday with Sabrina. When she finally gets up, there are fresh croissants on the bedside table, with fresh fruit and orange juice. She feeds Alex some of it, he feeds her, and then they take a long, hot, steamy shower together.

Making love in the shower would not have seemed possible before, not in the beginning. But they have become so aware of each other's bodies, so aware of one another's limitations, that nothing is impossible for them anymore. They bring each other to several orgasms with the spray from the shower beating down on them. Then they wash each other's backs and fronts and spend another few minutes kissing. They even dry each other and apply moisturizer on each other's bodies. They explore one another in new and wonderful ways, and they discover things about each other that they hadn't noticed before.

Sabrina has a mole under her left shoulder. Alex's birthmark is on his inner thigh. They point out these abnormalities on each other and look for the same abnormalities on the other person. Sabrina finds a mole under Alex's armpit. She tickles him, tries to pull a giggle from him, but he doesn't even flinch. He is not ticklish at all. He finds her birthmark too. It is in the strangest place you can imagine, and they both laugh at this. It is placed firmly on her thigh, on the back of it, right under her left butt-cheek. They spend the rest of the day discovering new and beautiful things about each other.

5

It has been six months since Alex met Sabrina in that restaurant in Jamaica. In these six months, they have gone from simply admiring each other to Alex giving Sabrina the chance of a lifetime, to curiosity, to being madly, wildly, insanely in love. Six months might seem like a short time, and it probably is to know for sure that you are in love with someone. Alex is confident, however that he has met his soul mate.

He needs to be sure, though, once and for all that Sabrina feels the same way. She has been present at every turn, fully present every time they have made love, and when they have been alone together, she has had nothing but love in her eyes. Sure, there have been challenges, from every corner, with everyone calling her a gold digger, and everybody thinking that Alex is going through a very erotic mid-life crisis.

Alex decides to get them away for a few days, just to get away from the storm that has become their social life. He knows that he took her away from everything that was familiar to her, everything that she knew. He knows that he expected too much from her and that she gave it willingly. Alex wants to reward her for this, to say thank you for everything that she has done for him, and with him. He wants to marry her.

They check into the beachfront Hyatt hotel in Hawaii at around six PM. It is a balmy Friday evening on the island, and they are both already sweating in the reception area of the hotel. Sabrina is wearing shorts that barely come over her thighs and a white tank. Alex is in board shorts and a t-shirt, making him look like a man trying to look younger. They get their share of stares, but nobody says anything. Of course, they know what everybody is thinking, but they are really beyond caring.

In the hotel room, Alex seems distracted. Sabrina notices this, and she wants to ask him what is on his mind. She thinks to wait a little bit before she asks him anything, but for the first time since they met, the silence is awkward. Sabrina does not know what to say to Alex to pull him out of the place that he seems to be stuck in, and Alex is not sure what to say to her, suddenly afraid of the response he might get to the question that is burning inside him.

Sabrina comes up behind him; he is sitting on the bed. She sends her hands underneath his t-shirt and raises it over his head. Alex lifts his arms, allowing her to remove the piece of clothing. She pulls her handbag closer, takes out some cream, squeezes a little onto her palms, and then rubs it together.

She places her warmed up hands on his back and digs deep with her fingers, drawing deep moans from him. He drops his head back, and then tilts it forward so that she can access his neck. Sabrina runs her fingers deep into the tissues of his thick neck, and he feels the reverberations of her touch right through to his fingertips. She moves back onto his broad back, and then up his neck again, and then she runs her fingers through his hair and massages his scalp deeply.

Alex closes his eyes as her fingers work absolute magic on his head. He loves the feeling of her fingers on him, and he really takes in every single sensation transmitted to his head from Sabrina's fingers. Then she pulls his head back and gives him an upside-down kiss. He kisses her back. They kiss in this position for the longest time, until his neck starts to take strain and he has to lift his head, tilting it forward so that she can run her fingers up and down his neck again.

Then she pulls him back so that he lies on his back. His knees bend over the side of the bed so that his feet are still on the floor. Sabrina comes around to his front and works his shorts off. She is grateful of the briefs he is wearing, so that they slip off his feet easily, making way for his shorts to slide down his legs with relative ease. She nibbles on his cock, still soft, underneath his briefs. It hardens almost immediately.

She pulls the white briefs off, exposing his thick erection. It always catches her by surprise, how large and firm her man's dick is, especially for his age. She knows that she is very lucky, but she also knows that she would have loved him even if his penis were less than average. You can learn how to make love; learn to work with what you're given. You cannot, however, learn how to love someone, not this way, not the way Sabrina knows in her heart that she loves Alex.

The briefs come off as easily as his shorts did. She takes his dick between her fingers, hoping to distract him from whatever it is that he is thinking about. She slips it between her lips and then eases the first few inches of it into her mouth. Sabrina moves her tongue into the eye of the thick snake, and moves it back and forth, and around and around. Then she works her mouth down the next couple of inches of Alex's meat.

She works her mouth up and down

on the tool, enjoying every bit of it, its length, girth, and taste. Sabrina starts to chew gently into the soft yet firm flesh of the mammoth rod, and Alex squirms with delight. She knows all his weak spots by now, and she manipulates everyone of them. She feathers his big balls while her mouth moves easily up and down on her man's dick. She loves that he loves it.

With his dick in her mouth, she places a hand on one of his knees to steady herself. Then she uses her free hand to remove her top, and then her shorts. She is happy that she is not wearing a bra, never needing too, her tits just the right size for gravity to have absolutely no effect on them at all. Age is also on her side, and so her breasts are full and firm, her nipples ripe and hard. She works her panties off, not once losing her mouth's grip on his firm dick, which is incredibly hard.

Alex has been hitting the gym hard in the last six months, mostly to keep up with Sabrina, but also just for his own health. It shows too, his stomach muscles firmer, the beginnings of a six-pack which he never had in his youth, and stronger, longer lasting erections.

This is the most enjoyable benefit, one that he does not know how he lived without. He had just been coasting from sexual experience to sexual experience before Sabrina, just getting hard enough for penetration, and staying hard enough to bring himself to a less than epic climax.

Now, though, things are very different. He has a fuller, firmer dick; it seems to be larger too by at least two inches. He knows this is probably just because his belly has flattened immensely, and so he knows that he has always had the length. He is happy, though that now he can, at least, see it, and exploit it to its fullest potential, with a woman he truly loves. Alex cannot remember feeling this way about any other woman before in his entire life.

As she mounts him, he remembers nothing of any other woman that he had been with before he met Sabrina. His focus is so completely on her now that Sabrina herself forgets even his state earlier. She too is no longer just trying to distract Alex, knowing that she has so expertly weaved her web of love on him now that he is present with her, at the moment, here and now. She too relaxes, ready for another epic round of lovemaking with her mature beau, which she too is completely in love with.

There is no need for condoms, thanks to Alex's vasectomy in his late thirties, and Sabrina has come to appreciate this. She knows that his erection would survive the minute or so that it takes to put on a condom, but she loves the feeling of his thick, long, naked dick moving around inside her. She raises herself above the aching rod, and then works her pussy over it, agonizingly slowly, but Alex has learned by now that he needs to let her make the necessary adjustments inside her cunt to accommodate him completely.

Inch by inch, Alex disappears inside her. He watches this feat, always amazed at how skilled she is with her pussy. She practically nibbles each centimeter of his dick into herself, and as thick and long as it is, it very quickly has less outside of her, then inside her. Suddenly all of his cock is parked quite solidly inside Sabrina, and she is moving each of her muscles individually over his meat. The feeling can only be described as incredible.

There is a moment where Alex goes into a daze, but just for a moment. This always happens to him when he fucks Sabrina, knowing that he has never had a woman like her before. He has never had someone so free of agendas, so eager to please him just for the sake of, and so besotted with him. He has never paid for sex, but with all the gifts he has given women in his lifetime, that is probably not the whole truth. Sabrina however, asks for nothing, expects nothing, but gives him absolutely everything.

He also has something for her, something small, but something that could change both of their lives forever. Alex is glad that he can trust Sabrina so much that he did not have to hide the engagement ring too much. He just put it in his shorts pocket, without the box, of course, his pockets so deep that he knows that there was no chance of him losing it. It is a massive rock, but she clearly has no idea what he wants to ask her.

Alex reaches for her firm mounds, and cups each one in his hands. He squeezes gently into the flesh, firm, solid but not. He runs his fingers over her nipples lightly, and then he pinches them, gently at first, and then a little more firmly. She places her hands over his and squeezes them so that he knows that he can give her nipples a harder squeeze. He does, and she arches her back, grinding her pussy harder on his dick, almost pulling it away from his groin.

Then she seems to place it back perfectly where it belongs and works her pussy in incredibly small circles on every part of his cock. She works various shades of magic on every inch of his hard meat inside her, using nothing but her cunt-muscles, and she sends every possible sense of pleasure through every possible part of his body. Even his fingertips have been turned into erogenous zones, his toes too. He starts to lose himself in the steady progression towards another grand orgasm.

Every orgasm that he has had at the mercy, or rather the grace, of Sabrina and her highly skilled pussy, has been magnificent. This one promises to be nothing less. She has a way of building up such a progression towards a climax that you would think she was conducting a massive orchestra or choreographing an elegant ballet. She always times it so perfectly that you would think she was able to read his mind.

Sabrina lets herself go just as soon as she knows that Alex is exploding deep within himself. They meet each other on the journey that they have been traveling together with their bodies, and they hold hands and fly off the edge of the magnificent waterfall of love. Sabrina falls onto Alex, face first, and their mouths meet. He turns himself so that he is on top of her now, still inside her, thrusting the remainder of his erection away.

They kiss for the longest time, and then he makes his slow exit from her pussy. He leaves her recovering on the bed, and goes to find his shorts. This is not how he had planned it, but everything has come together so perfectly that the timing just seems right. It seems to be the perfect way to seal off what has been only the beginning of an epic night of lovemaking. He digs around in his pocket and recovers the ring.

Alex brings himself up beside Sabrina on the bed and looks deep into her eyes. She notices that his distant mood has returned, and she wonders why. A million things start to go through her head, as to why he brought her here. Is this the end of them, she wonders? How can this be, though, when they have just made beautiful love, and he seemed so present throughout the process? She tries to shake this feeling from her, tries to free her mind of these thoughts, but it is futile.

Nothing has ever worked out for her, not in her entire life. She did not expect to meet Alex that day in the restaurant, and she had all but resigned herself to what she thought her life would be. Sabrina had a plan. She was going to work and save up money. She was going to attend a local nursing college. She was going to make something of herself. She did not expect to be Alex Ramsey's PA assistant, with a New York apartment, earning more money in a month than she would have made in a year at the restaurant back in Jamaica.

Her stomach knots, turning aggressively now, as Alex looks at her. She cannot help but think that she is going to lose everything that she has actually worked very hard to achieve. Sabrina wonders what Alex might say to her, how he might tell her that everything that she has will now be removed from her life. She braces herself for the announcement as Alex opens his mouth, closing her eyes, not wanting to see him when he tells her that what they have is now over.

Alex smiles; reading her nerves quite well. He kisses her closed eyelids gently, and she is even more confused. When he kisses her lips, she opens her eyes again, a million questions running through her mind. He raises his hand and answers with the appearance of the ring every single one of them. She gasps, unable to believe that in less than six months, Alex wants to marry her.

"Will you marry me, my darling Sabrina?" Alex whispers, knowing that he has now set her mind at ease, but also knowing that he has set a new string of emotions into play, which could be worse than her recent uncertainty and discomfort, depending on how she responds.

A smile starts to form on her face, as she begins to process what is actually happening here. Words fail her, and she cannot even bring herself to say that one little word that will set Alex's mind at ease. She pulls Alex closer so that she can reach his mouth easier. She kisses her response to him while Alex slips the ring onto her finger. It is a perfect fit, much to Alex's relief because he had the ring specially made.

Sabrina pulls away from Alex so that she can look at her finger. The massive rock sits perfectly on her digit, and a state of bliss overcomes her. He kisses her again, and she kisses him again, still speechless. He responds to her kisses with a massive second erection, fuller and firmer than his previous one, particularly now that he is more relaxed, and that she has responded the way he had hoped that she would.

Alex positions himself on top of Sabrina, still locked at the lips, and finds his way inside her a second time. There is a difference between making love to her now; he is not making love to his girlfriend, but to his fiancé. Alex sends his dick into her, slowly, but not as slowly as he allowed her to impale herself the first time, her cunt a little wetter, a little more giving. Soon he is all the way inside her, thanking her repeatedly for making him the happiest man in the world, with each full thrust.

He brings her to a beautiful orgasm, and then himself, and he falls on top of her, kissing her neck, whispering sweet nothings in her ear, a million *I love you's* making their way from his lips into the atmosphere of the room, which is balmy and heated, with every possible element of love hanging in the room. His fat cock remains parked inside his fiancé's soaked cunt, and he thrusts it inside her from time to time, reminding her that he has every capability of making her very happy, in every possible way.

They spend a wonderful week on the island, doing everything that tourists do, for Sabrina's benefit. By the time they fly back, there is a little bit of tension, not between them, but for what they know is waiting for them when they get back to New York. Now that they are engaged, this situation will be elevated to a whole new level, they know this, and they are not entirely prepared for the backlash.

All of Alex's friends have branded Sabrina a gold-digger. She knows this. She does not even blame them for thinking that she is, given the way things have worked out. From waitress to the PA of a self-made billionaire in two weeks, then getting into his bed a month later. Now, she is engaged to him, in less than six months, and she will be Mrs. Ramsey, Mr. Ramsey more than twice her age. She cannot say that this does not bother her either, since this was definitely not how she was raised, and certainly not part of a larger agenda.

She really loves Alex, for every reason possible. He is kind and considerate, and he pays attention to the small details. He really is very caring, and he listens to what she has to say. Alex takes her opinions seriously, and he acts on her advice when he needs to. There is something about the opportunity that he has given her too, an element of gratitude, but that is certainly not why she slept with him the first time or anytime after that. Alex is very attractive, and he wielded a power over her that she tried in vain to resist, for the longest time.

There is something in Sabrina that Alex saw too from the moment he laid eyes on her. He saw a fire burning in her eyes, which was subdued, needing the right moment, and the right man to ignite it. He is happy that he has been able to be that man. There is a deep satisfaction that he has within himself for being the man who has been able to unlock the young woman's potential, and now that she has agreed to be his wife, he knows that he will spend the rest of his life unlocking this potential.

Sabrina has ignited a fire in him too, one that he never knew was there until he met her. Alex was all about work, and about making money. He was all about building an empire, wanting to get nothing but material things out of life. Sabrina has taught him to appreciate the little things, to see things that he had previously taken for granted through fresh eyes, to really start to live again. He is grateful for this, extremely grateful, and he has really fallen in absolute love with Sabrina.

Alex arranges a dinner party to tell everyone the good news. He knows that it will not go down well with those in his circle, but he is too ecstatic to care. He pulls Sabrina next to him and raises her hand. The room goes silent, everyone taking huge sips from their champagne flutes, needing to fully comprehend how in just six months their friend has gone from bedding the help, to engaged to the *bitch*. They are clearly in shock.

"I know this may seem sudden to all of you...but when you know, you know...right!" He leaves this statement to reverberate around the room, and then he accepts the forced congratulations coming from the women in the room. The men seem to be focused on Sabrina, in a way that makes Alex a little uncomfortable. He knows that some of them have wanted to *eat from his plate* for a while now, but he also knows that they would not dare, would they?

After all, they have been warning him about Sabrina for the longest time, making her out to be everything that he knows she is not. He does not mind the women's scorn, knowing that the roots of this indignation come from feminine jealousy. It is easy to ignore it from them. The men, however, have been throwing their eyes Sabrina's way since he started sleeping with her, and this is a very dangerous game for them to be playing. Alex has never been able to share his toys, and Sabrina means much more to him than any trinket he has possessed in his life.

Sabrina has noticed this too, but she has ignored it for the most part. She had always been committed to Alex, even before they started sleeping together, and certainly, from the moment they officially became an item. She is really a one-man-woman, and she has her head screwed on straight. There are younger men who have given her unwarranted attention, and some older ones too, but this has not interested her at all. She has not even been flattered by the attention, viewing it as an inconvenience that she must just put up with while she solidifies her relationship with Alex.

Now, she has a wedding to plan, and she hopes, as does Alex that this will end soon. Sabrina is a little naïve, however; she does not realize the earnestness with which she will now be pursued by these vultures, now that the window of opportunity is closing, and she is soon to become Alex's wife. Alex is not so naïve though, and he knows that some of these men will probably up their game, pursuing his Sabrina with renewed verve.

Tonight, though, he does not think too much about this. He is focused on the love of his life, and the few real friends that he has in the room. He will keep an eye on the others though, and he will especially watch Sabrina, hoping in his heart, with everything that is in him, that she will not be taken in, and led astray, by the empty promises of these fools who want nothing more than to take a bite out of her *beautiful blackberry...*

6

It takes three months to plan the wedding, because of the international guests that had to move their schedules around to attend. Alex would have married Sabrina in the week after he proposed, if he had his way, but Sabrina insisted that they make this a networking event as well, so that Alex can engage with some of his international clients on a more social level, which would do wonders for his hard-core image. She has really proven to be worth her weight in gold.

Sabrina would have liked to have more time to plan the wedding, though, but with billions of dollars at her disposal, she really had no need to. Every detail was taken care of, and she seemed to be surrounded by people who were paid to make the entire experience of planning the wedding a little easier for her. She is as ready as she is going to be for her big day, and she is really looking forward to becoming Mrs. Alex Ramsey.

The marquee is set up on the beach of Alex's South Hamptons home. It is not a private beach, but with every other house so far from each other; it may as well be. Sabrina and her wedding party are at the house, getting ready, Alex and his groomsmen getting ready at a hotel in town. Everything is set up for a fantastic afternoon ceremony, and a night of incredible partying. The setup is magnificent, but Sabrina has not been able to bring herself to take a look, wanting to be surprised by everything.

She is very surprised when she finally steps out of the large terrace doors, and onto the pathway specially created for her, leading to an arch on the beach where Alex is waiting for her. She throws her eyes on the marquee, the sides up, the hanging floral creations blowing gently in the breeze. Sabrina looks at the tables, and sees that there are high floral creations on them as well; that seem to be reaching for the ones hanging from the ceiling. Everything is a light silver, infused with white, meeting and surpassing her every expectation.

The arch that Alex is standing under too has flowers decorating it, with similar hanging creations as are in the marquee. The priest is standing next to him, but Alex is the only man she sees. In fact, throughout the entire ceremony, her world becomes Alex, and she does not even know who she speaks to and who she doesn't. It really feels like a dream, one that she doesn't want to wake from. Every challenge that they have faced before this day seems to be a distant memory, like the autumn leaves of the trees that hang futilely hoping for new life, but then giving in, and falling away from the trees to make a place for new ones.

Reality sinks in when Alex carries her across the threshold into their prepared honeymoon suite, the master bedroom in the house taking a completely new appearance then the many times Sabrina has been here before. The room is bathed in candlelight, soft scents of vanilla and chocolate filling the space. He closes the door with his foot, and the whole world disappears. Even the crowd still on the beach enjoying the remainder of the reception fades into the background, the room filled with the husky tones of a female jazz singer that Sabrina has never heard before.

Alex carries her to the bed and places her on it with extreme care. He takes the two glasses of champagne on the side of the bed and hands one of them to Sabrina. They sip on the pink bubbles, and then he takes the glass from her. He kisses her, a grateful, passionate kiss that lets her know how he genuinely feels about her. She kisses him back the same way. They are both in the same world, existing in the same space, for the same reasons, from entirely different perspectives.

"I love you..." Alex says, meaning every word, every syllable.

"And I love you...more..." Sabrina responds, with the same sincerity, so that he believes what she is saying to him entirely. No more words are necessary, and they begin to disrobe one another, taking their time, like unwrapping a gift that you knew you wanted and have now received, but not quite believing it.

Naked now, they lie next to each other on the massive bed. They run their fingers up and down the length of each other's bodies, appreciating the prize that they have both won. Alex lays Sabrina on her back, and he admires every part of her body with his lips. She shivers at every contact, feeling the anxiety that she felt on the first night that she slept with him. She was no virgin, but she had also never been with a man like Alex before in her whole life. It is not even that he was the first white man that she had slept with, it was the way he actually paid attention to her, every part of her, and not just to the parts of her that he needed to slip himself into.

He shows the same attention to detail tonight, more even, the familiarity that they now have with one another plays a very important part in this. He kisses her down her flat belly, and he is glad that he has also put in the effort at the gym, making him more of an Adonis than he has ever been in his life. Alex knows that she will shower him with the same attention, given half the chance, but he is determined to show her how much he appreciates her first, letting her know that he loves all of her absolutely.

There is very little not to love about Sabrina too, Alex thinks to himself as he makes his way onto the soft curls covering her pussy. Her clit is so engorged though that is sticks out like a ripe fig that has split open in the summer sun. Alex kisses it gently, and then licks it tenderly so that it starts to sweat. The dew droplets forming on it are juicy so that Alex starts to lap them up hungrily, and then he kisses the soft, firm flesh again, as tenderly as he had just done.

He parts her pussy lips with his tongue and snakes his way into her pussy with his powerful licker. She holds his head, her fingers struggling to get a grip on his hair. Sabrina parts her legs a little more, bending her knees, willing him further into her pussy. She has started to drip profusely now, making it easier and easier for him to get further up inside her. He breathes deeply through his nose now, his mouth completely consumed with the task at hand. Alex was never one for oral sex, giving it or receiving it, but with Sabrina, he has discovered a new side to him that he knows that he will only ever explore with her.

Sabrina has an incredible orgasm. She wraps Alex's head between her legs and pulls him into her cunt a little bit more, as he sucks up her flow. He manages to drink up every drop of her juice, without once removing his mouth from her pussy. His tongue works its way in and out of her cunt, and then along the sides of it. When she finally recovers, releasing his head from her thighs, she is moist and ready for whatever else he has in store for her. She wants to love him too, but she knows somehow that he will not allow this, not just yet. He wants to love her in every way possible, and she will let him do just that.

He works his way up her belly again, dropping kisses on the line that he is tracing from her cunt to her breasts. When he reaches her firm mounds, he takes one of them into his mouth and sucks hard on the nipple perched on it, as though he expects it to give up milk. Alex moves across to the other breast, and sucks as hard on it, sending shivers down her spine, and culminating on her pussy so that it absolutely quivers.

There is an intense beating deep within her now, and she yearns for him to take her. She is used of his thickness now, but still, she has a little bit of apprehension about initial penetration. She wants this uncomfortable moment to be over quickly so that she can really enjoy her man, and so that he can enjoy her. She knows though that this will not be remarkably uncomfortable, and it certainly won't be as painful as the first time Alex fucked her with his exceptionally large cock.

After spending some time on her tits, he makes his way onto her neck. Then he finds her mouth, parting her cunt lips now with his fingers. He slips one inside her, and she receives the thick digit easily, knowing that this is not his dick, not yet anyway. He fingers her slowly with just the one finger while kissing her passionately before he adds a second finger to her cunt, which has now started to drip with moisture again. Alex pulls her closer and closer to a second orgasm, his dick throbbing now, wanting to find its way inside her, and needing to be enveloped in the power of her magnificent pussy. He will not rush this, though, needing her to enjoy every moment of this, their first time as man and wife, needing her to know what lies ahead for her, for the rest of her life.

Alex wraps his dick in the remaining fingers of the same hand that is working on her pussy. He knocks on her entrance, knowing that it is impossible for his cock to work its way inside her with his two fingers still firmly in place. He rubs his cock against her clit, though, and the beating intensifies both inside and outside her cunt. He keeps on doing this, and soon she is tensing up, caught in the throes of a second orgasm. It is even more magnificent than the first, and her pussy is considerably wet now.

He removes his fingers from her cunt and licks them hungrily. He knocks on her slit with a little more urgency now, really wanting to be inside her. She parts her legs a little more, trying to open herself up to him a little. He takes the gap, and slips the first inch of his cock into her hot, wet pussy, sighing a huge sigh of relief, even for this minimal invasion. He knows that it won't be long now, and he is glad for the beginning of what is always his best part of fucking her.

Slowly, very slowly, he starts to nudge his way into her. He returns his lips to hers, hoping to distract her a little from what is going on in her punani. It is hard, though, to ignore the insertion of this ramrod altogether, its thickness definitely not normal, and its length anything but average. Alex makes inroads, however, and soon enough he is in her cunt as far as his cock will go, as far as it can go. He gives her a moment to adjust, as he always does, asking her if she is okay, knowing the answer that he will get even before the question passes his lips.

"I am absolutely fine, my love," Sabrina says, with all the sincerity that she can muster. She still has fresh memories of the first time they made love, remembers how he could not bring himself to let her see his cock, and then spent a significant amount of time telling her that it was okay if she could not take him into her. The human body is a remarkable thing, though, able to adjust to anything if the intention and feeling is pure.

He eases his dick inside her, pushing against the involuntary resistance coming from within. There is something about knowing that he is too big for her that serves the masculinity in Alex very well. He has heard stories of black cock, and seen his fair share in the gym bathrooms and the occasional restaurant restroom, so he knows that these rumors were not totally unfounded. He knows, though, from all his past sexual experiences that he has an impressive dick, by any standards, something that has been both a blessing and a curse in his life. With Sabrina though, he is careful to make sure that it is an incredible blessing, for both of them.

Alex fucks her tenderly, with the patience of a saint. If she had thought that fucking him before was a treat, fucking him now that they are married is an even bigger one. She knows that she has to put her big girl panties on now, knows that she will have to go out of her way to please her husband. Alex is so gentle with her that he makes her want to do this, however. He makes her want to give him every experience that he has never had and elevate the experience that he has had. With each thrust, she realizes that she really does love this man, and she resolves to make the needed adjustments within herself to make sex for them as beautiful as she can.

He brings her to a magnificent orgasm, along with himself. He removes his dick from her dripping pussy just to refill their champagne flutes, and then makes love to her again. Each time they make love is different, unique, with twists and turns that make the trip down the garden path memorable. They talk for the longest time, and then they make love again. He has a surprise for her, and he knows that she is going to love it.

"I have a surprise for you, my love..." Alex says, loving the look of excitement in her eyes. "I have managed to clear my schedule for the next three weeks...and I'm taking you to the Caymans..."

This is a surprise. She had expected a honeymoon. She knows, though that Alex has only ever been able to get away from work for four days at the most. That he has managed to clear his schedule for three whole weeks must have really taken some doing. Sabrina is absolutely thrilled. "Three whole weeks...I'm not even going to ask you how you managed that...," she says.

"Don't..." he says, and makes beautiful love to her one more time before they both fall asleep in each other's arms, their heads filled with thoughts of their beautiful lives ahead, Sabrina asking herself how she got so lucky, and Alex doing the same.

They leave for the airport shortly after breakfast the next day. After a short plane ride, they touch down on the Grand Cayman Islands, arriving for the first time as Mr. and Mrs. Alex Ramsey. Sabrina cannot wait to change her name officially so that she can snap out of her dream state. She knows, though, somehow, that this surreal feeling will last a very long time. She has, after all, married the man of her dreams.

The couple arrives at the house on the Caymans shortly after midday. They are tired but not, energized by love, and the future that lies ahead of them. Alex is pleased that a full staff services this house for most of the year, even though he hardly ever uses it. It is mostly for the benefit of his friends, who can use it whenever they like. He hopes now that none of them decide to use it for the next three weeks. Alex doesn't think so, though, all his friends having been at his wedding the day before, and all of them knowing full well what his plans for the next three weeks are.

He goes through the list quickly in his mind, making sure that he told all his friends about his plans, hoping that they will exercise a certain amount of discretion, and stay away from the house that is essentially a holiday home for everyone. Alex knows that none of his friends approve of his relationship, and they definitely don't approve of his marriage. He cannot think of any reason for them to crash his honeymoon, however...he hopes they keep their distance so that he can spend the next three weeks loving his wife, and preparing her for her new life as Mrs. Ramsey.

"So, Mrs. Ramsey, what would you like for lunch?" Alex asks Sabrina once they have settled in.

"Well, Mr. Ramsey, I'll give you one guess..." Sabrina says, looking at her husband's sausage, already semi-hard under his shorts. Alex seems to have a constant almost-erection around Sabrina, always wanting to be inside her. They make their way to the master bedroom and make a delicious meal of one another.

Four days into the trip, however, they are in for a nasty surprise. Greg, Fred, and Tom arrive, unannounced, with three women who are young enough to be their daughters. Sabrina cannot judge them, however, but still, this is her honeymoon. Alex squints, questioning the three men with his eyes, unable to articulate the profanities that are ready to pass his lips. What the hell are they thinking? They were at his wedding, so they know of his plans for Sabrina, why then would they decide to just show up here, now?

Alex wants to pull them aside, to question them, and to kick them out. It is late, however, and so he decides that he will do it in the morning. One night with them will be a small inconvenience, one that he can bear if he does not have to see them. He decides to take Sabrina to the restaurant that they went to on their first trip, needing to create much-needed distance between himself and the men whose faces he wants to rearrange with his fists. They leave the three men to their own devices, after instructing the staff to put them in the furthest wing from the master bedroom.

"I'm sorry...you know how impossible they are..." Alex says, feeling the need to apologize for his friends.

"I know how they are, no need to apologize..." Sabrina puts his mind at ease just before Alex orders their favorite bottle of wine.

They have a relaxing dinner, talking until around 2 AM, not even realizing that the time has gone right by. Talking is the one thing they do better than making love, and they often lose themselves in conversation. Fortunately, tonight was one of those nights, and they get back to the house shortly after 3. Alex gets them a bottle of wine from the cellar, and Sabrina goes upstairs to get ready for more talking or making love, probably both. Without the pressure of having to be somewhere in the morning, nights and days hold the same magic, the same promise.

By the time they go down for breakfast later that morning, the conversation that Alex wants to have with his friends hangs like a white elephant in the room. After they have eaten, Alex finally pulls the men away onto the terrace, leaving Sabrina alone with the women who are all her age, but whom she has nothing in common with. She is very diplomatic, though, and while small talk isn't one of her strong points, she manages to keep them engaged while her husband deals with the little problem that these women are just an even smaller part of.

"You guys can't stay here. Not now..." Alex says, finally, after trying to be as diplomatic as possible.

"We'll be out of her in a couple of days buddy; it's just the only time that we could get away with...them..." Fred speaks for the group, pointing back towards the ladies with his head.

Alex really doesn't have the energy to fight with his friends, and he realizes that just a few months ago, less than a year, in fact, he was one of them, sneaking around the Caymans with whatever young thing had the ability to take his cock. He decides to let it go, just this once, and to let them stay for a few more days. Then they have to go, and leave him with his wife, accepting that he is now in a different league altogether, he is now a married man, and he has got to put his wife's needs before his friends.

Sabrina is not happy with the visitors, but she will have to take it in her stride. Alex has offered her assurances that they will be rid of the group in a couple of days, reminding her that they have two more weeks in the Caymans, so he promises to make it up to her. She is a little bit apprehensive about this intrusion, but she convinces herself that she will be able to handle it. She really has no choice now anyway, having said as much to Alex already, and knowing that she is not going to take it back.

By that evening, though, she wishes that she had not been so gracious. She did not want to come across as the new wife who turned into a bitch as soon as she got the ring on her finger, but now she regrets not being more assertive with Alex's friends. They are not her friends after all, and she knows what they want from her, what they expect from her, and she is in no way prepared to do any of it. She has no inclination now, nor has she ever had the inclination to be unfaithful to Alex. Now that they are married, this resolve is hardened, even more, set irrevocably in stone.

She stands on the balcony just outside her bedroom and looks down towards the swimming pool. Sabrina tries not to look, but when three grown men are skinny dipping with their bimbos right in front of you, it's kind of hard not to look. She looks back into the room when she notices that Alex is not by the pool, not wanting him to see her watching this scene. She remembers that he said something about having a call to make in the library, and then to respond to some emails before dinner.

When she returns her gaze to the swimming pool, Fred is looking right at her. He has a massive erection in his hands, holding it, rubbing it, holding her stare. It seems like he is calling her to him, urging her to explore his dick, promising her that she will be in for a massive treat if she will just let down her guard. She looks at this for 3 seconds, maybe 4, but the moment seems to be suspended, lasting forever. Sabrina turns away and hurries into the room, wanting to shake the image from her head, too late.

Alex comes into the room and notices that Sabrina is flustered. She puts it on the heat, and so he goes to open the windows that she closed on a reflex, wanting to keep the image, the penis, and its owner out of her bedroom, out of her head. The details of Fred's penis are printed on her brain now, and nothing that she does can remove this stain. She doesn't want it, by no means, but she does wonder what the fuck could have been going on in his head. She focuses on Alex, and his tool, taking the monstrosity in her mouth, between her fingers, and runs her tongue along the length of it. Soon enough she forgets what she has just seen, and soon enough her pussy is warm and wet, and she can take her husband into herself and forget the vulgarity that just occurred.

7

Sabrina tries her best to forget what happened last night. She puts it off to his friends having had too much to drink, and she just lets it go. It is hard, though because she is actually starting to be very scared of them. She starts to think that if she were left alone with them, that it might be a real problem. She decides to focus on Alex, to give all her attention to her new husband. There is nothing else that matters, nothing else that means anything to her so that she is suddenly very attentive towards him. Alex likes it. He likes it a hell of a lot.

After breakfast, thankfully just her

and Alex are at the table, she asks to be shown the island. She wants to see it from the local's perspective, and not as a tourist. Alex is too happy to oblige, hoping that when they get back to the house, their house guests will have left. They get into the open-top four by four in the garage and start their tour a little after 11. They plan to be gone the whole day. That should give the guys enough time to sleep off their hangovers and get the hell off the island.

The island is breathtaking, and everything that Sabrina sees reminds her of home. There is something about seeing things from the perspective of local people, the true inhabitants of a place that is very exciting. You become very excited by everything, and you see things that you wouldn't have seen before if you were just looking at things as a visitor. Visitor's eyes are tainted by the tourist management company of the places you visit. But immersing yourself in the lifestyle of a place gives you a fresh, new perspective.

It is this perspective that Sabrina looks at everything that they come across, and Alex sees things anew now as well, looking at things through Sabrina's eyes. He loves the world through her eyes. Things take on a different feel and a new interest. There is something almost childlike about this, and it really does make Alex feel a lot younger than he actually is. This does wonders for his self-esteem, and he really accepts that Sabrina is very good for him, and he is completely and absolutely addicted to her. This addiction is not bad too, but instead it sends new life into his veins, much unlike the effect of heroine.

As they continue on their tour of the island, he watches her more than the scenery. He sees her face light up at every turn. He just wants to take her face in his hands and kiss her. He is driving, though, so this is not possible. Alex makes a note to give her a big kiss as soon as the vehicle is brought to a stop. He looks around for a place where he can stop the car, but the narrow gravel road offers no such place. Then the road widens, and you can either go left or right. He goes right and comes to a cliff overlooking one of the many bays on the island.

He brings the car to a stop and then

he gets out. He goes over to Sabrina's side and opens her door. She gets out of the car, practically falling into his arms. Then he takes her lips between hers and kisses her deeply. He loves the taste of her mouth, the mixture of berries in her lip gloss, the slight musk in her mouth. There are traces of many flavors inside her, and he attempts to extract these with his tongue.

Alex works his tongue into the back of her mouth, over her tongue, and then underneath it. Then he runs his tongue over her teeth, before reinserting it into her mouth. Their lips do not part for the longest time, and when they eventually do, they are both looking deep into one another's eyes. He kisses her eyelids so that she shuts her eyes. Then he kisses her forehead, and then her cheeks. Returning to her mouth, he reintroduces her to the passion that he has in his own mouth, and the whole world does a swift disappearing act.

Then Alex throws his eyes around them, and he notices that you can still see the road from where they are parked. He thinks for a minute, and then he decides against doing what he is suddenly very inspired to do. He takes her hand and walks her among the trees. Then he finds the perfect little area, hidden from direct view, but offering them a glimpse of the vehicle so that they know they haven't gone too far. He suddenly wishes they had a blanket so that he could lay her down on the floor. Instead, though, he presses her up against a tree, and again he is kissing her full on the mouth.

Sabrina cannot believe that this is happening right now; right here in the open, but it excites her nonetheless. There is something about sex in public that has always been a turn-off for her, but with Alex, everything has a new edge. There is no turning back too, not when Alex has her shorts, and then her panties down to her knees. He looks at her pussy, and he parts the lips gently with his fingers. He licks the inside of her pussy gingerly.

Then he drives his tongue into her, deep and hard, and he laps up the juices that have started to rain down the inside of her cunt. There are few things that Alex finds more appealing than eating out Sabrina's pussy, and she knows this. She lets him, her hands firmly planted on the side of the tree. Alex really digs into her with his tongue, sucking out the juices inside her now, and swallowing every drop. Then he licks the outside of her again and plants his tongue firmly on her clit. He licks her clit gently at first, and then aggressively.

He parts her lips with his fingers again, blowing inside of her now, almost as though he is trying to blow out a candle. Then he kisses her pussy and reintroduces his tongue into her. Shards of pleasure work their way up inside her, tingling her belly and then into her chest, caressing her breasts almost. She looks up at the sky and then closes her eyes. There is nowhere for her to go, nowhere she wants to go. Sabrina wants to hold onto his head, but she needs the security of the tree just to hold herself up.

When Alex comes up to standing, and takes her top off, she looks around her again. She is completely naked now, and she is feeling very exposed. There is nobody around them, though, no signs of any life that are not natural to the surroundings close by. Sabrina just gives in to the moment, and she lets him do whatever he is doing, whatever he wants to do. He takes her breast into his mouth, flicking his tongue over the nipple, and then sucking on the whole tit. He gives the same treatment to the other one while working on his own shorts.

Alex manages to slide his shorts down, his underwear following soon after. He already has a huge hard-on, huge being the operative word. He opens his shirt down the front, but he doesn't take it off. He manages this with one hand. Incidentally, this is the same hand that is holding Sabrina's top. His free hand is moving over the breast that is not in his mouth. Then he moves this hand down her belly and onto her pussy again, fiddling with her clit, almost like he was busy with a light switch that just refuses to come on.

He goes into her with a single finger, stirring the inside of her, pulling the moisture down towards the entrance. When this juice starts to coat his finger, allowing it to move easier inside her, he adds a second finger. Then, after a moment, he adds a third, stretching her comfortably. She is really digging into the bark of the tree now, threating to pull it off. But she firms her grip on the trunk, and instead of pulling on the bark, she pushed down on it very hard. She starts to feel her knees weaken, and she hopes that he will hold her up with himself soon.

Sabrina cums, her knees buckling, and she places her hands on his shoulders quickly. The orgasm is so intense that she feels it in her toes, and up her calves. She feels it in the pit of her belly, and all the way up her chest, over her back and neck and into her head. He pulls his fingers from her slowly and replaces them very quickly with just the head of his penis. He too looks around now, hearing something in the bushes and needing to make sure that they haven't been caught out.

The island is very laid back, though. Nobody really cares what anybody else does, and especially the non-natives who own property on the island seem to get a get-out-of-jail-free card. So Alex really isn't concerned about himself, his only care is for Sabrina and her virtue. There will be nothing to explain if they are found in this position, and he knows this. He also knows that people are curious, inherently so, and so they will probably watch from the shadows. He has nothing to hide, though, very proud of his body, especially since he started at the gym, and he is as proud of Sabrina.

But she might not feel the same way about having an audience. So he makes sure that nobody is looking at them, although he cannot be 100% sure. He eases a little more of himself into her, turning himself a little so that he can block her from any eyes that might come around the corner. Then he feeds her a little more of his cock, and she holds onto his neck tighter. She is used to him by now, but that doesn't mean that this initial penetration isn't still a little uncomfortable.

He thrusts into her with about a quarter of his meat, and he really enjoys it. Then he eases more of it into her, Sabrina pushing herself down on his dick a little too. She wants him to get to that place where she knows he will not, cannot pass, so that she can settle into the actual art of fucking him, of making love to him, with him. He gets there sooner than she expects and she catches herself, bracing herself up on his neck, trying to lift her cunt off his cock a little, but it's too late. He is all the way up inside her, and she just has to try to relax into it.

When Alex starts to thrust into her with the full length of the meat that is lodged inside her, he practically lifts her off the ground. She comes up to her tip toes with every upward thrust, and then he eases her down on the outward motion. Over and over again he digs into her, raising her and then lowering her, elevating her to cloud nine, and then bringing her down to seventh heaven.

She has another orgasm, and then another, and then when Alex finally cums, she has another final one. He pushes her hard against the tree, digging some of the bark into her back. She does not feel this, her focus on the beautiful sensations between her legs. She cannot believe that he managed to draw so much pleasure from her, that he managed to bring her to so many orgasms in such quick succession. She holds on to his face now and pulls him down to kiss her. He kisses her beautifully while extracting himself from her dripping cunt.

He goes down to her with his mouth again, licking up the traces of her pleasure that escape her, and then helping her with her panties and her shorts. Then she drops her top over her hands again and pulls it down the sides. After he is sure that she is sufficiently put together, he pulls up his own shorts, along with his underwear. He leaves his shirt open, needing the coolness of the breeze to bring him back from the incredible pleasure that he has just had. Sabrina kisses him again, and then she takes his hand in both of hers.

"Thank you...and I love you!" Sabrina says.

"I love you too, very much...and babe, thank you!" Alex says, kissing the side of her face and then her forehead.

Then he walks her to the car and opens the door for her. After he gets in, he starts the car and leans over for another kiss. They are both sticky and wet, and they could use a shower. Alex drives down to the beach instead, though, and they find a secluded spot where they can dive into the waves naked. There is an almost relief that comes over them, washing over them with the soft whitewash of the surf.

They swim for a while, coming close to each other, kissing each other, disappearing underneath the water and then resurfacing, with their lips locked into on another again. Then they dry in the sun, before putting their clothes back on. They get dressed just in time too, because just as they make final adjustments to their appearance, a group of tourists comes around the bend and settles a stone's throw away from them. They walk down the beach towards their car, appreciating the openness of the all-terrain vehicle even more now.

After a short drive, they arrived in the town and chose a restaurant that has outside seating facing the water. They order drinks and then something to eat, and they settle into an afternoon of casual chatting and kissing. Public displays of affection are very high on the couple's list of things to do, and as a result, it takes them longer to finish their meal than it would have if they could keep their hands to themselves. They don't care about the looks that they are getting, both of them raising their ring finger unnecessarily, just to show everyone that cares enough to look that they are not just a couple of people stealing each other on the island paradise.

They stay for dinner too, not really wanting to get back to the house, not sure if they still have house guests. Alex thinks of booking them into a hotel, but then he thinks that this is very unnecessary, because the house that Fred and company have invaded is actually his. After dinner, and a few more drinks, they feel like they are comfortable enough to handle this bunch of intruders. Although both Alex and Sabrina secretly cross their fingers, hoping that they have had the decency to leave.

Alex and Sabrina arrive back at the house at around 10 PM, and they are immediately aware that they are still not alone. They walk through to the lounge area, the on that leads onto the terrace, with the swimming pool and Jacuzzi, and they see that every one of their house guests is there, half naked, and relaxing. They greet them, and then they chat to them for a while. Sabrina is really not in the mood for Fred and party, so after a brief conversation, and a polite decline of the invitation to join them, she goes to the kitchen, gets a bottle of champagne, and takes it to their room.

She closes the curtains, but not the doors; the heat is not allowing this. She waits for Alex to come back at any moment, and when he doesn't return for half an hour, she goes into the shower. When she comes out, Alex still has not made an appearance, so she moisturizes her body, and jumps into bed without opening the bottle of champagne. She will leave that to Alex when he finally decides to show up.

Sabrina wonders about his relationship with his friends, and she starts to think about how juvenile these other men are. How can they have such a hold on her husband? She thinks that it is probably because they have not accepted the man that he has become, still caught up in the nostalgia of days gone by. They were all probably bad boys in their day, and all of them, except Alex, have grown up since. This is strange too because they were all married before Alex. She wonders if Alex was as forward with their new wives as they seem to feel obliged to be with her.

Alex comes into the room about two hours later, and he looks a little more drunk than when Sabrina left him. She doesn't mind, though, knowing that this has probably got more to do with his friends than with his need to drink. He gets undressed and after kissing her again, goes into the shower. She thinks about the bottle of bubbles, and then she opens it, just because she can. When Alex comes out of the shower, she hands him a glass, and he joins her on the bed. He looks at her, and she at him, and then they burst out laughing.

They both know that this is not how they had planned to spend their honeymoon, and they know that the guests are just unnecessarily impossible. There is nothing that they can do about it now, though, except of course to chase them out of the house, but neither of them has the heart to do this. They will just ride it out, and then they will make up for it later. After all, they do have the rest of their lives to love each other and to be alone.

Sabrina decides in her head there and then to make more of an effort with Alex's friends. It will be hard, she knows this, but she will try. She has nothing to lose, though, and so this is what she will do. Alex is a little disturbed by his friends' behavior, though, and what bothers him more is that Sabrina has said nothing about this behavior to him. He wonders if it is because she is drawn to this attention, of if perhaps it is just because she feels like she can handle it. Either way, this bugs him, just a little. Actually, it bugs him a hell of a lot.

The bottle of champagne lasts them an hour, and then they relax into the large bed, making themselves comfortable in each other. There is nothing that can come and disrupt them in this space now so that they both fall asleep very easily. Nothing disturbs them either, not even the noise coming from the swimming pool. And it is quite a ruckus, with Greg, Fred and Tom playing around with their bimbos in the pool until long after midnight. Then the liaison takes on a more amorous nature, and none of them seems to feel the need to go to their rooms.

They just have a massive orgy by the pool, passing the women between them, so that you actually did not know where one body started and another one ended. You also didn't know who actually arrived with who, and it seems like none of them cared. It was just about sex, and sex is exactly what they were all having. Tom, Greg, and Fred were really the typical guys who flashed money and made panties drop. There was not a single pair of panties in sight now, though, and their shorts even were floating around the pool like abandoned pieces of driftwood.

Their other pieces of wood were working incredibly hard, though, mostly thanks to Viagra, but none of them will admit it, though, not to each other, not even to themselves. But the Viagra really did its work, and by the time they do make their way inside to their bedrooms, every cock has had a taste of every pussy, and they take the closest woman to them into their bedrooms, with no concern for whether or not they had arrived with that particular woman or not.

They have more sex than would be recommended for men their age, with that amount of drugs in their system, and that amount of alcohol, but they make it. They fall asleep quickly after, and they wake up around noon the next day. The sun is hanging high over the island, and they seem to have no intention of leaving. The women are awake already, though, and they have been up for a while already, giving the staff a hard time. Thankfully, Alex and Sabrina have already made their escape and are on the other side of the island.

The picnic that they have packed has everything in it. They settle onto the blanket that they made sure to pack this time, and Sabrina lays everything out for them. There are a few other couples on the beach too, and two groups of tourists, young, the picture of perfection, all abs, and beautiful breasts. Alex has eyes for one woman, though, and Sabrina only sees one man. They may as well be alone on the beach because they only have eyes for one another. They know, somehow, that it will be this way for the longest time.

Alex lies on his back, with Sabrina feeding him strawberries and kiwi pieces for breakfast, or brunch. They don't really know what time it is; they don't even care. They have the whole day to just sit and stay with each other, and to love each other. Alex opens a bottle of champagne, one of three that they brought with them, and pours them a glass each, before returning it to the chilling glove that it is in. Rich people really have found a way around everything, making their lives so convenient, that they never ever need anything else but what they have.

The couple really doesn't run out of things to say to one another, talking easily about everything that comes to mind. They discuss business and pleasure, and everything in between, and then they are silent, long, languid, comfortable pauses that hang in the air like ripe fruit on a tree, ready for the picking. The day moves easily from morning to early afternoon, and then early evening. The sun hasn't made any attempt to disappear from the sky, though, not yet, and so the beach is still well lit from above, even though it is nearly 7 PM.

By the time the sun sets completely, the two groups have started massive bonfires. They clearly have no plans of calling it a night anytime soon. Alex digs into their picnic basket, to check what they have left in it, what food they still have, and if they still have some bubbles. There is one bottle of champagne still, and two salmon steaks. He pulls them out, and decides that he will not start a fire for them; they will eat them cold, with this couscous salad that they still have left over. That is their dinner, and it goes down really well.

After they have eaten, they decide to make for the water. Nobody seems to be paying any attention to them either, everyone lost in their own worlds, seeing nobody but the members of their individual groups. Alex and Sabrina go waist deep into the water, and then they come closer to one another. They start to kiss, knowing where this is going almost immediately, so they go a little deeper into the water. Then Alex takes out his dick, unable to restrain it anymore in his shorts. He slips it out the slit in the front of it, trying to get it to hold up his shorts, succeeding eventually.

He loosens Sabrina's bikini bottom, held on by two strings on the side of it. He puts it in his pocket. There is no need for him to remove the top element, her tits hanging sufficiently out of it so that he can just pull them out into the open at will, and if need be, replace them snuggly in their covering. He removes one, and he licks the salty water off it. It fuses so perfectly with the lingering taste of champagne in his mouth that he feels like he is almost eating sushi.

Alex removes the other breast, and he licks the top of it slowly before he takes the nipple between his teeth. He turns Sabrina so that she is facing out towards the open ocean, and so that he has a clear view of the beach. He keeps his eyes on the people that are on the beach, and then he proceeds to devour both her nipples. They taste like a million beads of caviar firstly, and then they morph into soft bubbles of champagne. He couldn't have decided on a better after-dinner treat even if he tried.

Then he lifts her out of the sand and places her strategically over his scepter. He eases her down on himself, and then he works himself into her slowly. She kisses him deeply so that she is slightly distracted from his penetration. He gets all the way up inside her, and she tucks her legs under his butt. Then she lifts herself up off of him slightly, and then eases her way down him again. She is soon in a rhythm, and he just has to concentrate on keeping her up, so that she can bring herself, and him, to a beautiful climax.

They make love for the longest time; they know that it is long because the fires start to go out on the beach, and the people start to disappear. Then Alex helps Sabrina out of her hold and into her bikini again. He pulls her top up over her breasts and then he kisses her, sending fire into her mouth, as the fires on the beach start to fade and fizzle. By the time they are walking out of the water, there are just three couples left on the beach, all locked in love connections at the mouth.

After packing up their picnic they

head of the car, and drive back to their house. There is a brief moment of anxiety that overcomes them, thoughts of their house guests coming into their minds. They forget about them quickly, though, knowing that they have had a beautiful day, and knowing that nothing can happen now to take that away from them. Their love will see them through this, and as soon as time allows them again, they will take another honeymoon, and they will make sure that nobody knows where they are going this time, or for how long.

When they get to the house, it is a real party. There are people everywhere, and Alex has to bite his tongue. As if the three couples weren't bad enough, now they have about twenty people in the house. They cannot even escape them, having to go in and greet because as soon as the door opens, Fred looks over at them and calls them over to where he is sitting with another woman on his lap, a local. She really looks out of her depth, drinking champagne from the bottle. Sabrina is almost embarrassed for her.

"So, where have you kids been?" Tom asks, handing them both a glass of champagne.

They have no choice but to take it, and then they work their way down towards the pool, greeting everybody, not really taking note of the names that are falling from their lips. They all look drunk anyway, too drunk to even notice the nonchalance coming from Alex and Sabrina. They keep on looking at each other, trying to find the appropriate time to make their escape, but not finding a gap. It will obviously be a while before they can get away, so they both settle into conversations about nothing with whoever happens to be talking to them at that particular time.

Then Alex sits down, and he pulls Sabrina onto his lap so that all the other women present know that he is spoken for. They both lock their ring fingers around each other and make the diamonds on them very obvious. They hold this hand up often so that they don't need to say that they are married. It bothers them, though, both of them, that this is still something that they have to prove to anyone, even to this room full of strangers.

8

One by one the women make their way to the swimming pool. There seems to be no sense of self-control, or any inhibitions amongst this group, because they all throw their bikini tops by the side of the pool, and dive beneath the dark blue water. The men excitedly follow them to the water, and then they jump in after them. Shorts are flung in the air, landing with soft thuds by the side of the large swimming pool, and then the bikini bottoms are suddenly airborne. This is Alex and Sabrina's cue to leave, but Fred is suddenly behind them, with his shorts still on thankfully, and he is pushing them outside.

Alex reaches over and pulls a bottle of champagne out of the nearest ice bucket to him, and he lets himself and his wife be steered towards the swimming pool. Alex sits down on the furthest chaise from the pool, just to create a fair and acceptable distance between them and the pending orgy, also creating an easy escape for them the first chance they get. He pours glasses of bubbles for Sabrina and him, and then they lose each other in a conversation that has nothing to do with what is going on in front of them.

Flashes of dick and cunt come up to meet the open air before they disappear again beneath the water. Sabrina turns herself away from this spectacle, and she looks at Alex directly, and then through the large doors, watching the staff work irritably to sort out the mess that these impromptu house guests have made. She raises her hand, calling the youngest of the group of workers to her. After checking with Alex, she tells them that they can leave, and then they go, after thanking her profusely.

Then Fred and Tom come walking towards them, and Sabrina has nowhere to hide from their dangling penises. They lift her easily off of Alex and place her back down on the chaise. Then they grab Alex and pull him towards the pool. He fights them, cursing loudly, but also laughing so that they don't think that he is serious. They don't even pause when they reach the water's edge. Fred and Tom jump into the water, taking Alex with them, his shirt and shorts clinging tightly to him as soon as he is submerged. Sabrina watches in amazement, not sure what to make of this juvenile behavior.

Alex comes up, breaking through the surface of the water, and he looks around himself wildly, trying to find Sabrina in the darkness. When he sees that she is still safely on the chaise, he is almost relieved. She raises a glass to him, letting him know that she knows that this is not his fault and that it is okay for him to have a little fun with his friends. She cannot help but notice that most of the women are white, though, and those that are not, are the light-skinned yellow-bones that usually steal all the attention.

She wonders if there is anything that she should be worried about, but her intuition tells her that Alex really only has eyes for her. Even when some of the women come right up to him and rub their breasts on his chest and arms, she is strangely confident that his thoughts are with her. She watches as he makes his way out of the water, pushing these piranhas off of him as he makes his escape. When he is suddenly standing in front of her, she takes one of the towels by the side of the pool, and she helps him dry off.

He takes off his shirt, and she works the towel over his chest and then his back. She wipes over his cock and is surprised by the size of it again, making her stop, just to evaluate it. She gives it a firm squeeze and it hardens slightly. Sabrina loves the fact that she has this effect on him, and when she goes to her knees to dry his legs, Alex has a fully established erection. There is just something about her on her knees between his legs.

Alex takes the towel from her, and then he leads her into the house. He ignores the wolf whistles coming from behind them, knowing that it is just to aggravate him. He will not be aggravated by this bunch, and besides, he has something else on his mind, walking behind Sabrina up the stairs, kissing her back, kissing her ass, kissing the back of her legs. Tonight he will make to absolute most of her body, and she will show him everything that he has inside him. Something about making love to her on a bed makes him think of a painting on a canvas, and his dick is the paintbrush.

When they get to the room, Alex locks the door, not trusting his friends tonight, knowing that mischievous look in their eyes that he has seen in the past, and it has not ended well on any of those occasions. So just to be sure, he locks the door and then checks to see that it is indeed locked. He appreciates his staff when he sees a bottle of champagne in an ice bucket, with two glasses and a bowl of strawberries. He makes a mental note to tip them and thank them in the morning.

He works Sabrina's clothing off her, and then he takes off his own shorts. Then he kisses her all over the side of her neck, and her face, and then he practically swallows her mouth. She notices one thing about him now, something that she hadn't paid attention to before, but with them moving on her directly right now, she notices that he has nice full lips, not like any white guy that she has seen before. She has never kissed a white man before, other than Alex, and she has certainly never been with a white man that way, but Alex is everything that she never even knew she wanted in a man.

Alex really feels like he will never tire of making love to Sabrina. Every time he touches her, every time he sees her naked in front of him, he has new and wonderful ideas as to how he can please her. She is so receptive too to all his suggestions that if he had not become a master at reading her body, he would think that she was just agreeable to these suggestions because she didn't want to make him feel bad.

He lays her on the bed and kisses her up the full length of her body. Starting at her toes, working up her calves and then planting gentle kisses on her knee, and then he kisses her thighs, and settles briefly between her legs. Then he kisses the sides of her belly and settles for the longest time on her breasts. He licks, kisses and then sucks on them, and then he bites into her neck. After what seems like a beautiful forever, he reaches her mouth and lingers there longer than he had on any other part of her.

Alex works his way back down to her toes, and then up to her mouth again, over and over, each time planting kisses of varying pressures and intensities on her, making her feel like her was running a feather over her entire body, and then making her feel like he was planting soft suckers on the parts of her that his lips find. It is beautiful, and she relaxes into this deluge of kisses without even thinking of doing the same to him. This isn't necessary, not yet, and so she just lies back and enjoys it.

She feels his fingers creeping up her inner thighs. Sabrina parts her legs now, wanting his fingers to reach her aching cunt quite quickly. When he does, she breathes in deeply, literally smelling the scent of herself coming up out of her pussy. She never smelt herself this way before, and she knows that it is probably because she is so incredibly aroused. For a brief moment, she is conscious of it, and she is slightly embarrassed. But when Alex puts his nose directly on her snatch and takes a huge sniff, she knows that it is okay and that he loves it very much.

Every time the curtains blow into the room Sabrina throws her eyes towards them, trying to see who might be on the other side of the windows. She knows that it should be impossible for anybody to be on the private balcony, but with the sounds coming from the swimming pool and entering the room, she starts to feel like she is being made love to in full view of everybody. Again she tries to relax, and she closes her eyes as Alex continues to sniff around her pussy. When he eventually parts her lips with his fingers and runs small circles on her entrance, she is right back in the moment with him.

His tongue enters her with the stealth and aggression of a serpent. She arches her back in response, feeding him a little more of her pussy, swallowing more of his tongue with herself. He fucks her gently with the full length of his tongue, and then he licks the outside of her pussy hard. Alex works his way onto her clit, pulling it between his teeth and lips, and then pounding hard against it, using nothing but his tongue, over and over again.

Her orgasm feels like a sunrise over the ocean. It comes over her in waves, gently hitting the shore, swelling ever higher and higher. She sees it coming, but still it hits her by surprise when it finally arrives. It consumes her so aggressively that she almost resembles someone having an epileptic seizure. She shudders and shakes for a very long time, so long that Alex begins to worry himself. But then she starts to calm down, and he moves his fingers over her entire body, bringing her gently over the cliff that makes up her magnificent climax.

Alex hangs his heavy cock over her head now. She reaches up and takes one of his massive balls in her mouth. She sucks on it, nibbles on it gently, and then after he requests, bites into it a little harder. She moves on to the next one, giving it the same treatment.

Then Sabrina licks the entire surface of his nut sack before she tries to take both his huge balls into her mouth at the same time. This is not possible, though, but she does put forth a valiant effort. Then she resigns herself to just taking them into her mouth one at a time.

He points he dick towards her mouth now, using his hand. She goes for the head, licking it first, and then nibbling on it too. Then he eases about two inches of his thickness into her mouth, and he fucks her gently with just this small taste of his cock. He eases another few inches into her wet mouth, and after adjusting her head, she takes it easily. Alex knows to be careful now; otherwise, he will impale her through her throat into the bed. There is a moment where he wants to try for more, though, but he knows somehow that he has stretched her mouth as far back as it will go.

Then he also starts to feel the beginnings of an orgasm. He is so predictable when he is about to cum, and she takes note of his signature moans, groans and grunts. She prepares herself for the flow that will erupt at any moment from his massive volcano. At any moment now, a sea of hot lava will spew out of the tip of his cock and into her mouth. She must be ready for this excess, or risk having to change the sheets. She adjusts herself a little more, and then he blows, coating the back of her throat excessively. His seed is warm and almost sweet. She loves the taste of her husband, knowing that she will probably not be as willing to swallow any other man's load.

"Nice…" Alex says, looking at her in her eyes now, and then rolling off the bed to pour them some champagne.

"Very nice…" Sabrina responds, smiling uncontrollably. She has learned a lot about herself in the time that she has been with Alex, and she really appreciates the lessons that she has learned, about herself, and about the male body.

They sip on their bubbles, and chat easily about their houseguests now, laughing at the banter coming up to their room through the glass doors. They hear Fred mostly; he is the most vocal. He is also the most recently married, and the woman that he has come with here is certainly not his wife. Fred's wife is beautiful too, the daughter of a Texas oilman, very old money. What she sees in Fred is beyond the comprehension of both Sabrina and Alex. They discuss Tom and Greg too, and also their wives. There is no gossip here, just concern for these women who seem to be too content to leave their husbands to their own devices.

Alex gets up and goes over to the doors. He pulls them closed, drowning out the sounds somewhat, but not completely. At least now Alex and Sabrina can hear themselves think, and at least now they can focus on each other completely. They drink the remaining liquid from their flutes, and then Alex disposes of the glasses. He returns to the bed, and immediately kisses her on her neck, and breathing in her scents.

Then he takes her lips in his, and he kisses her as his cock hardens and then goes soft a bit, hardening quickly again. He wants in now, but he is just enjoying the taste of her so much. Sabrina is the one who actually initiates penetration now, though, and she takes his dick in her hand. Then she holds it against her pussy, not pulling it into her, instead, pushing herself up into it. She gives way easily, and a few inches of him slip into her. Then she lets go of his cock and eases her pussy up and into him.

He doesn't even move himself now, just holding himself in place above her. As she lowers herself down a little, he follows her, and then pause, letting her work more of her pussy over his meat. When it goes as far as it will, he doesn't move at all. Sabrina grinds herself against him, and he feels the pleasure of this movement in every part of his dick. He feels it into his balls even, and he takes a moment to get used to this feeling. He has fucked her many times before, but this is the first time that she has shown so much initiative.

Alex cannot stop himself from thrusting into her now, and he moves his meat around inside her, three-thirds of him, and she takes it. She takes all of it and starts to really get into it. He rubs his cock against one side of her pussy, and then the other side. This is really just a transference of pressure, his meat stuffing her quite thoroughly. She really loves this feeling now, and with time, she has come to really look forward to it. She knows that he can fuck her forever without cumming, and now, tonight, that is exactly what she wants.

She gets that and a whole lot more. Alex makes love to her beautifully for most of the night. He sends himself into her over and over again, and then he lets her rest as soon as she has had an orgasm. Then he starts thrusting gently into her again, bringing her to another orgasm. When they finally fall asleep, they are both exhausted, and they are more in love than they were when they started making love. They are more in love than they were last week, and certainly more in love that they were when they first met.

Breakfast is bearable too, since most of their houseguests have left, and the rest are still asleep. Fred, Tom, and Greg are still here, though, but this doesn't bother Alex and Sabrina so much. They start to plan their next honeymoon, not sure even if they should mention possible locations out loud. When Tom comes out of his bedroom and down the stairs naked, they know that they are in for another very long day. They sigh, and then kiss each other. Together, they can face anything, even Tom walking into the dining room with his cock still semi-erect, looking confused.

9

Alex and Sabrina go outside to the pool, already dressed for a swim. Sabrina looks at the water, and then she looks at Alex. He seems to read her mind because he calls the pool boy over and instructs him to drain the pool and clean it. This will take about half the day, so they take a walk through the back gardens and onto the beach closest to them. It is still early enough in the morning for the beach to be deserted, although it is not a private one, and so Alex and Sabrina settle down on towels and read the books that they brought with them.

They hold hands, and lose themselves in their reads, and then they kiss each other, just to remind themselves that they are in love and in this shit together. It really is shit, they think, and they know that it will not be over until they are off this island and away from these fuckers who intruded so blatantly on their honeymoon. That is beside the point, though, and anyway, it is not important right now. The only thing that matters is the two of them here and now, together.

After a while, Sabrina thinks of getting some snacks from the house. She looks over to where Alex seems to have fallen asleep. She doesn't blame him; he really worked her last night. It was absolutely beautiful. Actually, it was magnificent. She still feels him between her legs too, even though it has been a good couple of hours since he exited her. Sabrina kisses him on his forehead and then whispers "I'll be right back" in his ear. Unsure if she has been heard, she gets up carefully and makes her way back up to the house.

Sabrina gets to the terrace and walks up the steps to come face to face with Greg, Tom, and Fred. Their women are looking at the emptying pool, looking like sad puppies actually. Sabrina cannot help but smirk. She says good morning to everybody without stopping, walking straight through into the house and to the kitchen. She chats briefly with the two maids she finds there and then she packs a picnic basket. She remembers that there is no sunscreen on the beach with them, and so she puts the basket down and runs upstairs.

She finds the tube on the counter in the bedroom, and as she turns to leave Greg is standing in the doorway. Here we go again; she thinks, and she asks him with her eyes what she can do for him. Greg just looks at her up and down, and he smiles. She is really not in the mood for this, not now. Her husband is on the beach; a stone's throw away, and even if he wasn't, she is a married woman. There is really very little respect for her marriage in this house, and she starts to really hate it.

"So, Alex huh..." Greg asks her, although she isn't even sure if it is a question.

"Yes, Alex!" she says, and she tries to push past him after taking the sunblock off the counter.

"What is it about him?" Greg pushes, running his fingers over his penis now, an obvious erection forming!

"I am really not going to discuss my husband with you, Greg, now, if you'll excuse me!" She tries again to push past him, but he plants himself firmly in the doorway. Then he walks into the room and closes the door behind himself, keeping it closed with his body.

"Then let's not talk..." Greg says, putting his hand inside his shorts, threatening to pull his erection out into view.

"I really don't have the time for this or the strength. Get out of my way Greg!" Sabrina tries for her sternest voice, and she looks him directly in his eyes. She catches a glimpse of his penis now; he is really pulling it out. She turns into the room and looks out of the window. She really doesn't have the strength to push Greg out of the way, and she certainly doesn't have the stomach for his dick.

"Come on...you know how we are...all of us... Alex is no different. We take what we like, whenever we feel like it...and then we forget about it, and go on with our lives. I'm not asking you to do anything that Alex wouldn't ask of my wife!" Greg sounds like he actually means every word, as he believes himself. Sabrina really doesn't know what to make of this situation, and she turns around to face him again. He is completely naked now, and he points his penis at her directly.

She shakes her head. Then she goes to the bed and sits on it. Greg comes up in front of her and then sits beside her. She sees a gap, and she takes it. After dashing for the door, she is glad that he did not lock it. It gives way easily, and she makes it out of the room before he has put his shorts back on. He follows her out into the hallway, but Sabrina is already halfway down the stairs. She goes to the kitchen and takes the basket off the counter, and leaves through the backdoor.

When she reaches Alex he is still sleeping, and she kisses him on his mouth, needing him to wake up. He opens his eyes, surprised that he fell asleep, but even more surprised at the picnic basket. He doesn't realize how long he has been asleep, so he just shakes his head and tries to get his bearings with the time. She kisses him again, and then she unpacks the basket, happy that she thought of everything. They settle into a beautiful brunch, forgetting about their books for the moment, forgetting about everything but each other.

There is something on Sabrina's mind, though, and she thinks that she is going to tell Alex. She thinks that she might just let him know what his friends have been doing, what they have been saying. What if though, just what if what Greg said was true and Alex would ask the very same thing of his wife. What if this is just the way they are, the way they will always be? This thought settles in the pit of her stomach like a volcano threatening to erupt. She cannot get her head around anything that has just happened, around anything that has been happening.

She looks at Alex, the questions hanging in her eyes. He sees this and asks her several times what is on her mind. She lies, of course, and says 'nothing', and then she kisses him again. They eat, and feed each other, and then they sip on their champagne. It is obviously never too early to start drinking on the island, and so they really enjoy the bubbles. It is also a good thing that the house never seems to run out of champagne either like there are little elves who stock the cabinet and the fridge in secret every night.

When they make their way back up to the house shortly after lunchtime, the see that everyone is around the pool again, still looking like they could sleep some more. The pool is pristine, and it beckons Sabrina to dive into the water. She looks at Fred and Tom, though, and then at Greg, and she decides that she will not swim now, nor at any time during her honeymoon, not it this swimming pool, and certainly not with these men as her audience. She goes inside and sorts some lunch out for her and Alex, and then she takes the food upstairs, where she finds Alex coming out of the shower.

"I'm going to go downstairs for a while, just so that they don't feel like I'm neglecting them!" Alex says, referring to his friends as though they were five-year-olds who needed watching.

"They really shouldn't be here..." she says before she can stop herself. She looks away from him, gathering up the makeshift picnic that she set up on the master bedroom's terrace. When she looks at Alex, he isn't looking at her, looking instead down towards the pool, looking at his friends who really have no place here.

"I know babe... I promise to make it up to you." Alex promises as if it was all his fault that his friends were such jerks.

"Don't worry about it. Go down and spend some time with your friends. I'm going to shower and have a little bit of a siesta." She really doesn't want him to feel like he is forced to choose between his friends and her. She promised herself early on that she was not going to be that kind of girlfriend, and certainly not that kind of wife. He helps her take some of the plates and leftover food downstairs, and then kisses her, watching her walk up the stairs before he goes out to join the party by the pool.

After about a half hour under the water, Sabrina dries herself and moisturizes. Then she goes onto the bedroom terrace and looks over to where Alex is locked in a ruckus with Tom and Greg. She doesn't see Fred, so she goes to lock her bedroom door. She will think of a reason for this later when Alex comes upstairs if he meets with the locked door. However, he seems to be settled into the afternoon's chatting with his friends, and she needs to make sure that she will not have to put up with any of the nonsense that she has put up with until now.

She gets on the bed, nothing on but her light robe. It falls off her legs, and off her pussy, and she is happy for the breeze coming through the windows. There is no way for them to see into her bedroom from the pool, so she feels safe, letting herself hang out like this. Sabrina reads her book a little and then falls asleep soon after. Her robe falls off her breasts too now, and she looks every bit like a centerfold.

Tossing is a habit that she has had her whole life, and although she sleeps in one place mostly when she is Alex's arms, she knows when she is alone in bed, and the tossing demon takes her over again. There is nothing to keep her on either side of the bed either, so she really makes the entire bed her own. The robe gathers above her butt now, and she lies on her back, her breasts perfectly mounted on her chest and heaving up and down steadily as she breathes in and out.

She stirs suddenly. Sabrina feels she is dreaming, the breeze blowing the curtains into the room in slow motion. The sun is setting too, and the colors of this sunset play in the sky, licking the balustrade on the terrace. She thinks that she can make out the outline of a man, but this is impossible. The door is locked, isn't it? And there is no way for anybody to get up to the terrace, except through the bedroom. She closes her eyes again, certain that she is just imagining things.

Then something tugs at her, and she opens her eyes again. She strains to see in the dark, although the room is lit generously from outside. She catches the outline of a man again, on the terrace, with his hand on his penis, which is fully erect, from what she can make out as the curtain blows out of the way. She is suddenly very alert, knowing that she isn't seeing things, and knowing that this man is definitely not Alex. She pulls her robe over herself as quickly as she can, and then she sits up in the bed.

Fred is masturbating furiously now, close to her so that she can hear his grunts. She can see that his eyes are closed now, having adjusted to the contrast between light and darkness. She cannot pull her eyes off his penis now, and she watches as he erupts, catching the escaping semen in his hand. Then he pulls his shorts up over his dick, wiping the seed off of his hand on his shorts. When he opens his eyes, he looks into the window, and he sees Sabrina looking at him. He is not even embarrassed.

He turns away from her and walks over the terrace, disappearing over the edge. She is not sure what just happened, and again she thinks that she is just dreaming. Fred cannot have jumped from the second floor of the house, onto the pool deck. She gets up to go and see where he is, and what this actually means for him. He cannot fly, she knows this, and so the curiosity of this situation forces her to go towards the door, step out of the window and onto the terrace, and towards the edge of it. She needs to know what happened to Fred.

The explanation for this is very simple actually. There is a ladder up the side of the house, just an arm or so away from the edge. There is a creeper growing up over it so that she knows why she did not see this before. She looks down at the pool and sees Alex asleep on one of the pool chairs. He is probably passed out, so she knows that he is probably unaware of what Fred just did. She cannot help but pull the robe tighter over herself, thinking that he must have had quite a view, for the longest time, before she woke up.

Sabrina thinks that they must even have come up and watched her make love to Alex. This is really a strange world, and the complete absurdness of it finally settles on her, so that she is aware at last that she is in a whole new world. In this world, women are traded like stocks. That a woman can say no to these men is not even a thought on their minds, and they certainly seem unable to take no for an answer. She hates that she is so completely thrust into this world and that if she wants to get out of it, she will probably have to lose Alex. This is something that she cannot even consider, though.

She walks back in the room and unlocks the door. She needs to fetch Alex from downstairs, knowing that he has drank too much, and knowing that nobody else will care for him, leaving him to sleep uncomfortably on the deck chair. She turns back halfway down the hall, realizing that she is still naked for all intents and purposes. She throws on a summer dress, minus underwear, and goes to get her man.

On the terrace, she meets Fred's eyes first. She shakes her head at him when she sees him smirk at her. She goes over to Alex and is surprised when he wakes up before she even touches him. He looks at her and then looks around at the darkness, surprised that he has slept so long. She helps him to his feet and then helps him inside without saying anything to the other people on the terrace. She walks him upstairs, and then after getting him comfortable; she goes back downstairs to make him coffee.

Sabrina has never seen Alex quite so

drunk. His friends really have a very bad influence on him. She wonders how it is, though, that someone so mature, so in control of everything in his life, can let himself be controlled by 40-year old juvenile delinquents. It's probably a white thing. Or maybe it's a middle-aged thing. She doesn't know. And she didn't care until tonight. But, truth be told, she does care. She cares when it turns her man into a puppet for the amusement of these idiots. This is something that she will have to address.

Addressing this situation is the last thing on her mind, though because Greg is standing in the kitchen when she walks in. He comes close to her quickly and grabs her arm. Sabrina wants to pull herself away, but it is not possible, his grip firm. He pulls her towards him and kisses her neck. "Fuck off," she says. She tries again to pull herself away from him, but he is insistent, sucking hard on her neck now. Sabrina manages to pull herself away from his mouth, though before he manages to pull a love-bite to the surface.

"Stop fucking playing hard to get

dammit... Trust me, it's okay. Nobody will mind!" Greg says, trying for her mouth but landing on the side of her face.

"I'm not playing at anything. And I'll mind, that's all that matters. Now leave me the fuck alone!" Sabrina surprises herself by how aggressive she is; how absolutely authoritative she sounds.

Greg takes her hand and puts it directly on his erection. She tries to pull it away, but again, he is insistent. He rubs her fingers up and down the length of his tool, and it is quite impressive, she has to admit. But she still doesn't want to be touching him, not like this, not in any way actually. She just needs to get away from Greg, but she realizes that getting away from him right now before she has said what is on her mind will be pointless.

When Greg moves her hand down his shaft again, and she gets close to his balls, she yanks her hand from him and takes his balls between her fingers. She gives the orbs a firm, resolute squeeze, and then she twists to the right. After twisting in the other direction, she pulls down hard. She is still holding his balls tightly in her grip.

"I said leave me the fuck alone. If you don't, then I'll be forced to tell Alex. We'll have to see how little he minds..."

"Oh, he won't...trust me... do you like what you feel?" he asks her, obviously in pain, but looking past it at the almost-erotic nature of this encounter. She lets go of his nut sack and pulls her hand from him at last. Then she goes to the coffee machine and pours a cup for Alex. She looks at Greg, wanting to say something, feeling the need to, but caught off-guard by how confident Greg is that this will not bother Alex.

She hands him the coffee when she gets back upstairs, looking at him, wondering how much she really knows about this man. She wonders if she did not rush into marriage perhaps and if maybe, just maybe, this swinging setup that has been suggested to her at every turn is just the way these men operate. If this is the way they handle their relationships, though, then this is certainly not what she signed up for. There are just a few things that she will not accept as a part of her life.

After Alex has had his coffee, he has a quick shower. Then he jumps into bed after brushing the taste of alcohol out of his mouth. Sabrina watches him fall asleep easily, after kissing her for a while, but obviously too drunk to take things any further. She watches him sleeping and her mind races with everything that has happened so far on this trip. She thinks of her encounters with Tom, Fred, and more recently Greg, and she wonders what the fuck is really going on here. Could Alex really be in on this game that they seem to be playing with her? What if she gave in to this, not that she would, though, would Alex really be okay with this?

She falls asleep, thinking of this, and of many other things. There has got to be a way for her to get to the bottom of this situation, without alienating Alex from his friends. If there is, though, she cannot think what it is just yet. Sleep certainly doesn't come easily, and she is very confused, more so that she has ever been in her life. She cannot believe that her life is suddenly so riddled with complications.

When they wake up in the morning, Alex is already kissing her before she even opens her eyes. They make love well into the morning, the covers having fallen off the bed completely now, and the two of them rolling on top of one another over and over again. Now he is on top of her, thrusting into her gently, and then she is on top of him, riding his dick gently, easily, until she comes to an orgasm. Then he is thrusting into her again, bringing himself to a beautiful orgasm. Then he goes downstairs to get them breakfast, and coffee, him needing it, Sabrina too.

Sabrina gets up off the bed and goes to the window. She pulls the curtains open and walks out onto the terrace before she realizes that she is still naked. Something catches her eyes, out of the corner, and she turns to look at where the ladder comes up over onto the terrace. She catches the remainder of an arm, someone climbing down the ladder again. This person, whoever it was, was watching them, the whole time. She hates this. She feels like screaming. Before she can, though, Alex comes up behind her and puts her robe over her.

"Careful my dear...we have rather randy houseguests. And the sight of you is enough to drive any man wild!"

He turns her around and kisses her, then walks her inside and they have their coffee and breakfast.

She looks at him, reading more into what he has just said than is actually there. She hates this sense that something is happening to her that she is totally unaware of. Sabrina hates the fact that she is suddenly a part of something that she isn't even sure of. After breakfast, she gets dressed without showering and takes the breakfast tray back downstairs. Alex is left in the room, lying on the bed, waiting for her return, ready to go again. Sabrina looks out onto the terrace to see who is there, trying to make sense of the disappearing arm off the terrace. But, seeing nobody there, she has to question if she really saw what she thinks she did.

10

Sabrina feels incredibly exposed, but she does not know how to tell Alex what has just happened. She thinks that maybe, just maybe, it was all in her imagination, but she knows in her stomach that it was not. How little Greg must think of her, how little Fred and Tom must think of her. They have made it very obvious what they want from her, and she has not even thought about any of them that way before. Even in light of everything that has happened in the Caymans too, she still does not think of them like that. They are Alex's friends; that is all. She resolves that they will never be hers, though, even if they apologized for their recent behavior.

"Are you okay, honey?" Alex asks Sabrina, noticing that she has something on her mind.

"I'm good babe," Sabrina says, not looking at Alex, thinking that he will be able to read right into her, and see what she has just witnessed.

"Are you sure?" he presses. "I'm sorry about...this...I really did not think that they would come...or that they would stay, especially when they realized that we are also here..." Alex apologizes for his friends.

"It's okay...really it is...it's your house and they're your friends." She tries to suppress the urge to throw up, remembering the site of Fred, masturbating right outside their bedroom window, remembering the look on his face.

"It's our house, my love... and we could have just told them to leave...we can still tell them to leave..." Alex offers, even though they have one day left of their honeymoon, and the first flight off the island will only be in the

morning again.

"I'm fine...really," Sabrina tries to convince Alex, but he knows her much better than that. He also knows not to press her for an answer, guessing correctly that someone or a couple of *someone's* did something inappropriate, again. He resolves to sort this out once and for all when they get back to New York. For now, though, he has to focus on making their last night in the Caymans memorable.

He starts to kiss her on her neck, and on her back. He starts to remove her robe, but she holds it over her breasts and throws her eyes towards the open curtains. Alex reads her mind, although he wonders why tonight, on their last night here, she has a problem with their open curtains. He closes them, though, without asking her what has got her spooked. Alex thinks he knows, though, and this really angers him. Now is not the time for him to be angry, though, and he returns his focus to his new wife.

She lets him remove her robe now, and stands naked in the room with her husband. She looks at the door,

wondering if it is locked. She hates that she is suddenly so paranoid, and knows that she must just snap out of it, or risk having to explain her discomfort to Alex, which will really ruin their honeymoon; although, how much worse it can get, for her, then it has already been so far, she cannot see right now.

Alex is wearing speedos, the outline of his erection already forming underneath them. He had asked her to join them in the pool for an evening swim, and now, in retrospect, she wishes she had. It is too late to take back the events that have just unfolded, though, and so she determines to try to shake herself free from this memory. The best way for her to do that is to focus on the man in front of her, her man, the man she married, the man she loves.

She gets onto her knees and takes the speedos off her man. His cock falls against her face, and she is brought immediately to the moment, knowing that she needs to really concentrate now. Sabrina takes his dick in her hands, able to fit both her hands on it, with a good three or four inches ending

in a massive head. She points this head at her mouth, and works her mouth on it, and then over it. Sabrina takes the first few inches in her mouth and sends her tongue in circles around the huge dome.

She does not close her eyes, wanting to be present in the moment, to forget the sight of Fred's dick, the sight of his fingers moving up and down on it, faster and faster, and the look of lust in his eyes. She remembers Greg and Tom too. She moves her hands further down his shaft, taking more of the dick in her mouth. Sabrina licks the meat in front of her like an ice-lolly, and then nibbles on it like a very hot corndog. Her eyes start to glaze over, and she is lost to the man that is in front of her now, completely.

Then she places one hand over the other, intensifying her grip, and she works all of the cock that will fit in her mouth into it. The stretch is incredible, and she loves it. He also loves it, especially when she takes the fingers of one hand and wets them in her mouth, and then places just the tips on his balls, feathering them fast and furiously, in clear contrast with the

slow, intense way that she is sucking on his shaft. She is very good at sucking cock, and Alex hopes that she learned this skill by working on his meat.

The idea that his is the first dick that she has ever had in her mouth is absurd, though. He knows this. He only hopes that his is the first dick that has ever received this much attention from her beautiful mouth. It is a very beautiful mouth, he thinks, as he watches her lips wrapped tightly around his thick dick, moving slowly up to his head, and then down on his shaft to her fingers. Her tongue joins the party too, and her teeth; and she makes a meal of her husband's penis.

He gets close to having an orgasm, and so he holds her head to stop it from moving. He doesn't want to cum just yet. He wants to please her too, and he wants her to have as good a time as she is ensuring that he is having. He watches her work on his meat a little bit longer, and then he lifts her up off his cock and brings her up to her tiptoes so that he can kiss her on her mouth.

Alex kisses Sabrina while walking

her back towards the bed. When they get to the bed, he lifts her off the ground, effortlessly, and places her on top of it. He kneels next to the bed and pulls her towards him so that her legs rest on his shoulders. He takes her cunt into his mouth and works his tongue along her slit. Her lips part, her clit is immediately full and flowered, and he sends his tongue into her pussy with the energy of a bull.

He brings her to an orgasm before she realizes what is happening. She knows that this is his idea of foreplay, getting her pussy wet and ready for him, and so she lets it happen. She squeezes his head between her thighs, oozing her cunt-juice into his mouth. He licks his lips, and then licks her pussy on the surface, not wanting to remove her natural lubrication from the walls of her tight cunt tonight. He cannot resist getting into her quickly, so he knows that he will need all the help that he can get.

Alex turns her over, and pulls her off the bed slightly so that she is also kneeling beside the bed. He places his hands on her asscheeks, and parts them to reveal her tighter, more closed asshole. He wets the hole with his tongue, and she shakes, unable to control herself. Sabrina is grateful that her knees are on the ground, and she is grateful for the rug under her knees, comfortable in the new position, relaxing enough to give her ass to her man completely now.

He really goes for her ass now, sending his tongue into the tight hole, fighting for entry, insisting on it, though. The hole eventually starts to give, so he manages to get his tongue inside her asshole, and she lets out a loud moan. Alex knows that he has her now, and he relaxes into his enjoyment of rimming Sabrina, something that he knows for sure he was the first man to do to her. He loves that he was her first *something*, especially sexually.

He reaches around underneath her and finds her pussy. He pulls on her lips and pinches her clit. More goo oozes out of her snatch, and he rubs it along the surface of her hot place. Then he sends a finger inside her and finds her hole hot and wet. His cock starts its signature throbbing, and he knows that he will not be able to hold back much longer from entering her.

Alex does manage to extract another orgasm from his beautiful wife, though, and she cums so hard that her thighs are drenched in her warmth.

Lifting off her asshole, he sends a finger into the tight hole that his tongue just occupied. He fingers her asshole slowly, gently, with just one finger. Then he adds another finger and watches as her ebony hole swallows his fingers easier and easier. The temptation to send a third finger into the hole is too much for him to resist, and so he holds her in place and very slowly adds a third finger. Then he fingers her steadily, knowing that he will not bring her to orgasm in her asshole, although he wishes it could; maybe one day!

After the longest time, he removes one finger. He continues to finger her with the two fingers, and then slowly, he removes another one. With just one finger left in her asshole, Alex pulls her away from the bed slightly, and then he positions himself underneath her. He holds his dick, and points it directly at her pussy, readying himself for entry. He really cannot hold himself back anymore.

Alex finally removes his finger from her asshole and pulls her lower down so that his cock makes contact with her cunt. His solid tip is primed for entry, and her pussy is so wet now that he is comfortable taking her in this position. He pulls her onto his cock so that she is almost sitting on it, and he slips the first two inches of his meat inside her. She braces herself, but he is in no hurry for full and complete monopolization of her pussy, not just yet. He thrusts into her with just these two inches, holding her in place, moving her up and down, adding another two inches very slowly.

She would gladly just sit on his meat, and then adjust to this intrusion, but he has his hands on her firmly, controlling every inch that he is working into her. Soon enough, though, he has disappeared into her, almost completely, but he knows that this is all that her tiny pussy can take. He lifts her up off his dick partially, and then sits her back down, lifts her off, and then sits her back down, sending half an inch more inside her than the first attempt. Thrilled by what he has achieved, he starts to move her around on his cock, working them both towards climax now.

Alex pushes her off his cock a bit, just so that the tip of it is still inside her. He comes up on his knees completely, pushing her back on the bed a little more. He brings himself up behind her, and drives his dick into her again, almost all the way. He starts thrusting now, really thrusting, and he reaches under her and takes firm hold of her breasts, giving them a good solid squeeze as he rams his now purple-headed warrior into her quivering pussy. He loves this position, and he knows that she does too.

He also appreciates the rug under his knees now, as he plants his knees firmly in the soft angora beneath them. She too is comfortable in this position, and he is really ramming into her now, giving it all his got. Many things could be going through their minds now, but they are both really just enjoying each other. Nothing that they could be doing now solidifies their love this way. They are really wrapped up in one another now, in a way that they could not explain even if they tried.

They both come to climax in this

position, ending with Alex giving one final confirming thrust. He manages to lift them both up onto the bed with his dick still lodged inside Sabrina. Alex is on top of Sabrina still, with her lying on her stomach. He thrusts slowly now, in and out of her wet cunt, ensuring her complete satisfaction, but also getting her ready for another round. Even though his dick softens a little, he does not mind. She also appreciates the relief, knowing that it will not be long-lived.

Alex sends his arms under hers, and then places his hands on top of Sabrina's, holding her firmly in place. He drives his resurrected erection into her depths, hitting the far reaches of her pussy now, going where only he has ever gone before. He fucks hard, having built up incredible momentum quickly. Sabrina's cunt literally weeps with each full entry of her husband's massive boner. She bends her knees slightly, unwittingly giving Alex uncompromised access to her punani now.

He rams into her, grinding his dick into her now, moving his hips in large circles, using every muscle in his buttocks to send himself completely into Sabrina. Her pussy has given way completely now, resistance is both futile and impossible. She is absolutely stuffed with dick now, and this draws from her another great orgasm. Alex is nowhere near climax, but he manages to maintain a firm hard-on throughout.

Even when he removes his dick from Sabrina, it is still rock hard, and he wonders if she will let him try for a little ass action again. The last time he tried, it did not end very well. He takes to her asshole with his mouth again, though, sending his tongue into the tight space again, checking to see how receptive it will be to another attempt. If she cannot take it, though, he will certainly not force her.

He digs into her asshole with an intensity now that lets her know what he wants. Immediately she clenches, squeezing the shit out of his tongue. Still, he maintains his composure, showing his characteristic patience. As soon as she relaxes her hole a little, he sends more of his tongue into it, and then almost immediately is victim to its incredible chokehold. He takes a deep breath and keeps his tongue moving steadily in and almost out of the space, enjoying the clenches now; hoping secretly that tonight will be the night that she lets him have her asshole.

Alex removes his tongue completely now and replaces it immediately with two fingers. Her hole receives the fingers easily, but soon it wraps so tightly around them that Alex thinks immediately that this must be what it feels like to be stuck in the grip of an anaconda. His patience and persistence pays off, though, and soon enough he is moving four fingers in and out of her asshole. He removes the fingers completely and then reinserts them. Again, he removes them, and again the fingers slither their way into her. Soon enough, he is getting all the way inside her ass with four of his thick fingers effortlessly.

Then he removes his fingers entirely, and places his dick directly on the hole. He braces himself up on his hands, and nudges his dick back and forth on the hole, with no indication that he is going to enter it, just teasing her with the tip of his meat. Alex puts a little more pressure on the hole, and Sabrina opens her legs, bending her knees, and raising her ass slightly. Alex's head disappears into her asshole, catching him by surprise so that he stops nudging. Is she actually going to let him take it tonight?

He thrusts a little bit inwards and is surprised when his dick slips into the hole almost halfway. Then it is wrapped in the chokehold that his fingers enjoyed earlier, and he thinks correctly that he might have gone too deep, too quickly. She breathes deeply, hiding her face in the pillows to muffle her moans. She knows that Alex really wants this, but she also knows that if she is not enjoying it, then he will stop. She really wants to satisfy him in any way possible, the same way that he has always satisfied her completely. She also knows, from what she has read and heard about anal sex since the last time Alex tried it, is that you just need to get past the first few minutes of discomfort, and then you will see the pleasure to be had from it.

Sabrina does not move. She just lets Alex know that it is okay with a soft whisper. He pulls his dick out of her a little bit, and then drives an inch of it back into her. He fucks her slow and steady with just this inch, and once she relaxes into it, he sends another inch into her. He keeps on adding an inch into her after she becomes comfortable with the last few inches she has accepted. When he gets to half of his meat inside her, there is no way for her to take any more. Alex is very grateful for what he has been given, so he commits to enjoying it thoroughly. Enjoy it he does, wishing just that he can bring her to a climax as his own appears over the horizon. He needs to stay propped up on his hands, though or risk sending more of himself into Sabrina, something he knows she is certainly is not ready to take.

He eases his dick into her asshole now, slowly, deliberately so, until half of his dick is lodged inside the tightness. Then he starts thrusting into her with this part of his dick, and he is thrilled with this. She feeds him a little of her ass, surprising him a little, but not too much. She always does something to surprise him, but this was certainly a first. He stops thrusting, letting her ride his dick with her ass from below, allowing her to do what she needs to make this easier on herself. Soon enough more of his dick is swallowed by the black hole, and he resumes his thrusting, certain now that all is well, and that she is comfortable with this entry.

Reaching underneath her, he inserts three fingers into her pussy, continuing his assault on her ass. He brings her to a final orgasm, and himself too, and then he slowly eases himself out of her hole. Her ass snaps shut again, despite the painstaking effort he put into making this as painless as possible, and then he pulls her to him, kissing the back of her neck and her hair, breathing her in. They spoon for the longest time, and then they turn towards each other, and have a casual conversation about their love for each other.

The three men downstairs also have a conversation. They talk too casually about Sabrina's resistance, totally oblivious to the fact that she may just really be in love with Alex. They cannot believe that he loves her too, convinced still that he is just going through a midlife crisis, and that soon, when he is over it, that he will move on, and leave her high and dry. They must get a taste of her, though, soon, if their appetites are to be satisfied. They must have Sabrina, break her resolve to stay faithful, to prove to themselves that she is nothing but a gold digger, and that, given the right opportunity, she will give in to their advances, moving swiftly along to the next best offer.

But what could be better than Alex though, they ask themselves. Yes, they are all successful in their own right. This success, however, has been largely on the back of Alex's success. They know this. She probably knows this too. So money will not be enough for them to lure the beauty into their beds. They also know, from many shower locker-room sessions with Alex, that their dicks don't come close to his, and so they know too that this is not going to work. What can they do to get her over to the dark side now, they ponder, literally salivating at the thought of having Sabrina.

Alex is not stupid, though. He has seen the attention that they have been giving to Sabrina. They have certainly crossed the line; he is sure of this. He knows that they have made their advances known to her, but what her response has been, he does not know. He needs to be sure of what her thinking is, or has been about this situation, but since she is not saying anything about this, he really doesn't know what she is thinking.

He thinks that maybe he should just ask her about this. He thinks that he might ask her now, on the last night that they are in the Cayman's so that he can get to the bottom of this once and for all, and know what to do going forward. He goes downstairs to get a bottle of champagne, not so much for the atmosphere, but more for him, to bring out the questions that he has to ask her.

Watching her drink her wine, though, he is torn. He really loves her, deeply, truly. But he isn't sure if she is really in love with him. He thought he was sure while they were dating, and he was even sure when she agreed to marry him. But he also knows how they met, and the circumstances that really brought them together. Could all his friends actually be right about this situation? Is she possibly just a very good money-sucker? Is he, in fact, going through a midlife crisis, one that sees him drawn to a woman who should actually want nothing to do with him, for historical reasons?

Alex questions very little in his life. He makes a decision, and he sticks to it. This is how he has always been. He has also managed to go after and always get what he wants. So why is he suddenly doubting himself? Is it because he feels like he so aggressively pursued her, that he did not give her time to figure out her feelings? This is possible, he reasons, but he really hopes that he is wrong. He cannot accept that she was forced into marrying him, that she felt that she had no choice in the matter, simply because of the opportunity that he gave to her. How can he know for sure, though?

He watches her longer. There is something seductively vulnerable about her, even now, even after the long time she has spent submersed in his world. He cannot bring himself to question her about this, afraid of offending her. He could not handle it if he was the reason that she suddenly felt uncomfortable with him. She is not the one at fault here after all, and so he resolves to sort this shit out with his friends, as soon as they get back to New York.

Sabrina is also thinking about this situation, sipping carefully on the champagne in her hand. She thinks about telling Alex about the incidents that have happened in the last few days. She thinks, though, that if his friends are right, then he will see her as stiff and a bit of a prude. Sabrina knows, though, that if indeed they are right, and Alex will not mind her being passed around among his friends, then she will definitely need to rethink this marriage. How did it come to this, though, she wonders?

She wonders a lot of things actually. She thinks about the incidents that she has had thrust upon her since she married Alex, even before, and she thinks of the details of these events. What is it that they hope to achieve from this behavior? Could it be that they are just really actually just this way? If so, how could it be that they are so successful in their daily lives if this is how they handle their private affairs? Is this lifestyle just their way of rewarding themselves for their successes?

Sabrina hates that she feels so anxious now, even now, with Alex. Yes, they make love, and yes, it is beautiful. Yes, he says all the right things, and she responds to him easily, and honestly. Could he just be playing her, though, like a fiddle, like a guitar, or like a well-tuned piano? There is nothing that can rip her way from these thoughts either, so she is stuck in her own head, not even knowing that he can see that she is lost in thoughts. He notices this, and he knows why, but he has no way of protecting her from what has already happened. He resolves to make it better for her, going forward, though. He isn't sure how yet, though, but if he is meant to lose his friends in the process, then so be it.

She doesn't know what he is thinking either, and this makes her anxiety even worse. When Alex comes up to her and kisses her, she drops her glass to the floor, shattering the crystal. She looks down at the broken glass and bends to pick it up. He pulls her to him, though, so that she knows that she should just leave the glass where it is. He looks at her deep in her eyes, promising her without words that all will be okay, very soon.

Sabrina thinks again that she should just tell Alex what is going on. But then she realizes, as he kisses her neck, that if this is all a game to him, she will not like the response she gets. She thinks that she will handle it on her own, finding a way out of this situation, whatever that way is. She does wonder, though, as Alex works his fingers up her leg and between her thighs if she is prepared to walk away from Alex if he is indeed just playing a very elaborate game with her.

11

For two whole days after they return from the Caymans Sabrina is distracted with thoughts of what went down with Greg, Fred, and Tom on the island. She is consumed with thoughts of everything that has played out before even her wedding, and she is torn between telling Alex, and preserving his friendships. She hides her distraction well from Alex though, and he does not question her.

What she cannot believe, though, most of all is the utter disrespect that they have shown for her relationship, her marriage, and ultimately her man and herself. Did they really expect her to fall so quickly for their tricks, probably discussed over drinks at the club, or in the shower at the gym? She can only hope that they will get the message now, but she knows somehow, that this torment is far from over, not by a longshot.

"Can I help you?" she asks Fred, who is standing in the doorway to her bedroom in the New York penthouse she shares with her husband.

"I'm looking for Alex..." Fred says, looking at her exposed thigh, her robe falling carelessly off her leg as she moisturizes her long, chocolate legs.

"Well, obviously he is not here..." she responds, not really having the energy to play nice anymore.

"Obviously," Fred says, rubbing his hand across the erection forming in his pants already.

"Not this again, Fred... It is never going to happen! I think you need to leave..." Sabrina looks at him in his eyes, although he is trying to draw her attention to his cock.

"Are you sure?" he asks her, attempting to see under her thin robe, hoping for a glimpse of her place between her thighs where her treasure is hidden.

"Sure about what?" Alex asks, appearing behind Fred suddenly.

"I was looking for you... we need to discuss Tokyo!" Fred says, not skipping a beat, adjusting his dick and then turning to face Alex, walking him back down the hallway of his own apartment. Fred is a nasty blend of arrogance and cockiness.

Sabrina finishes getting dressed, and leaves the penthouse, after kissing her husband on his mouth. She looks at Fred, hoping that he will get the message, and leave her alone. If not, then she will continue with the public displays of affection, until everybody leaves her the hell alone, and allows her to enjoy her marriage and her new husband. She heads out, meeting a few friends for breakfast.

Fred on the other hand, cannot get the thoughts of Sabrina out of his head. He keeps his hand on his crotch throughout his meeting with Alex, trying as best as he can to hide his erection. When he finally cannot take it anymore, he sees an opportunity, Alex on the phone, and goes into the bathroom. He whips out his dick quickly, knowing that he doesn't have a lot of time to pleasure himself, but also knowing that he needs to cum, or risk exploding.

He looks around the bathroom for some sort of lubrication, and, finding none, he wets he palm with some spit from his mouth. He takes his cock into a firm grip and moves his hand quickly up and down the length of his shaft. His mind goes immediately to Sabrina, to the vision of her thighs, and his imaginary vision of what her cunt must look like, what it must taste like. He brings himself to a swift finish and manages to catch most of the semen escaping the tip of his cock in his hand.

Fred takes some toilet paper and wipes his hand, and then cleans the tip of his dick. He washes his softening cock in the washbasin, and after drying it, returns it to his pants. Then he washes his hands, and after checking that his cock is placed perfectly inside his trousers, he exits the bathroom and returns to finish up with Alex. His satisfaction is incomplete though, and he resolves to consult his black book, just after his next meeting, to see if there isn't someone in there who resembles Sabrina. He knows, however that he will find nobody in there that comes close to Alex Ramsey's wife.

After his meeting, around one-thirty, he reaches into his glove compartment and pulls out his black book. It really is a black book, a small diary, with the names, numbers, and brief descriptions of his most recent *sexcapades*. Fred is also a married man, but this does not bother him. He fucks his wife enough for her not to care that he is fucking everything in a skirt that finds him even mildly attractive. Fred also likes younger women, but he never thought that he would be interested in a black woman. He admits to himself that he really just wants Sabrina because she belongs to his arch nemesis, Alex Ramsey.

Fred remembers a college student that he fucked a few months earlier, a film student from Dallas. She had a roommate, if he remembers correctly, a black girl who wasn't very attractive, but she will do, for the purposes of his current fantasy. He knows that the student was eager to please him, something that he found a little off-putting, but she had a hot body, and he needed to fuck. He wonders as he takes out his cell phone, how he can convince this eager beaver to meet him at the apartment he keeps in the city for the sole purpose of fucking. He wonders how he can convince her to bring her friend with her as well.

A terrible combination in any major city is having no money and daddy issues. Anne, the film student, has both, and fortunately for Fred, so does her roommate. Tina, the roommate, got all the details of Fred and his performance from Anne just hours after they fucked the first time. She was curious about him, intrigued even, if the stories that Anne told her were true, so it doesn't take too much convincing for her to join Anne and Fred for a little mid-afternoon fucking.

The girls arrive at the apartment and find Fred already naked, drinking. The door is open, so they walk straight through, straight into a naked Fred. He offers them a drink, and Anne is quick to accept. Tina takes the glass from

Fred, without once taking her eyes off his cock. He notices the intrigue, lifting his cock up, shaking it around for a bit, and the rubbing the head gently. She looks at Anne, and then goes down on her knees and takes the tool in her mouth. She sucks on it excitedly, so excitedly that you would swear that she has not had sex in a long time.

Fred carries on a casual conversation with Anne while Tina gets him hard. The situation is so casual that you would swear that they had all done this before. Fred pulls Anne towards him, and after downing his drink, he sticks his tongue deep into her mouth. She kisses him back after getting her footing. Then she downs the remainder of her drink, Tina's too, and she returns her lips to Fred's. Tina has him rock-hard now, and he is ready for some serious fucking. He looks down at Tina, still working her mouth on his meat, and then he looks at Anne, holding her just far enough from him so that he can look at her face.

He pulls Tina up off him, and he kisses her too, moving his mouth between the two women. He works their clothing off with both his hands, his lips working on their necks and breasts, and then back to their lips. When both of them are naked in front of him, he turns them around, over and over again, like mannequins on a revolving pedestal. He really likes what he sees, and he is more intrigued by Tina's pussy, hidden carefully beneath soft black curls. Black women obviously have no desire to make their pussies look like baby's bottoms. Or maybe it's just Tina. He wonders if Sabrina's pussy looks the same.

Fred searches under the curls with his finger, trying to locate her clit. When he finds it, he presses down on it, hard, and she moans. He repeats this, sending her into a moaning frenzy, and then he watches her face. Her eyes are closed, her mouth pulled to the side slightly, so that he knows that she is anticipating more. He gives her more, sending his finger into her as soon as he finds the entrance to her. Tina's lips part easily, and he works his finger almost all the way up inside her. She takes it, all of it, and when she settles comfortably on this one finger, he carefully adds another.

Anne is not neglected either, two,

and then three fingers in her perfectly shaved pussy. He digs into both women, deep, and he really likes the fact that both pussies are wet, aching for him to take them. Fred likes to be wanted. He likes the feeling of security and control that this gives him. Both women fall on to the sofa right behind them, and his fingers dig deeper and deeper into them. They start to moan loudly, so loudly that he suddenly wishes that he had two dicks so that he can satisfy both women simultaneously. However, he hasn't evolved that much, not yet, and so he has to choose who to enter first.

The choice is obvious, though, and he positions Tina just right. He enters her quickly, and thrusts into her hard, with enough room to work because of how he has positioned her on the couch. His balls hang low behind him, and Anne positions herself so that he can take the orbs into her mouth every time he thrusts out. He fucks her with his eyes closed, his thoughts on one woman. He cannot bring himself to open his eyes once, and Tina watches his eyes closed, wondering where exactly he is.

He appreciates the feeling of wetness on his balls, and so he lingers on the outside of Tina, letting Anne work well on his balls for a moment longer before he pushes his dick back onto Tina's depths. Harder and harder, deeper and deeper he sends himself into her, bringing himself closer to climax. He cannot even think about Tina's satisfaction now, because, in his mind, he is fucking Sabrina. He goes into her for a few more swift strokes, and then he empties his cock into her. He can only hope that she will have the sense to visit the pharmacist in the morning, because unlike Alex, he has not had a vasectomy.

When he pulls out of her, he is tired, but not too tired not to give Anne her dues. He fucks her too, quickly, and he seems to enjoy this session more than his previous one. Tina notices this, and she notices also that Anne has an orgasm, unlike her. She takes her fingers to herself and brings herself to an end, nobody in the room noticing that she has had to sort herself out. She puts on her clothes and leaves the apartment, closing the door behind herself as Fred cums hard into Anne, fully satisfied now.

Fred pours himself another drink, and he looks at Anne lying on the couch, drained. He thinks to himself how easily these young women can be lured into his lair, but how the one woman that he wants here still eludes him. He calls Greg and Tom, to discuss this situation. Tom is a little apprehensive; having made peace with the fact that he will probably not get Sabrina, not after their time in the Cayman. He is also a little concerned about Alex now, not sure if Sabrina has said anything to him about their behavior.

Greg and Fred are determined to still, though, sure that they just need to dangle the right carrot in front of the woman, and she will eventually bite. Fred fucks Anne once more before making some excuse about a late meeting. There is no need for him to even make this excuse, though because Anne knows the position she fills in his life. She is just convenient pussy to the middle-aged man, nothing more. She accepts this role, made easier by the $1000 that Fred palms her along with a goodbye kiss.

Fred paces the apartment, still naked, waiting for Greg and Tom to arrive. They arrive about an hour later, to find him still drinking, still no clothes on. He has no problem being naked in front of these men. He has no problem being naked in front of anybody actually because he is very confident about his body. It is a decent body too, so there is nothing to hide. And he seems to love the freedom that being naked in this apartment affords him. His home life is stiff and rigid, and so he makes full use of this opportunity.

"What does he have that we don't?" he asks Greg and Tom.

"Sabrina!" Tom answers, rather candidly. Both of them look at him, and they shake their heads. Then they look back at each other, thinking that Tom seems a little bit distracted. They decide to ignore him, thinking that he is probably getting cold feet. This is no time for second thoughts, though, so they decide to work on their plan alone. If Sabrina doesn't want one of them, then maybe two of them will be better than one. They just need to get her alone and get to the bottom of her resistance.

It is actually rather sick of them, but they don't care. They want to get to Sabrina, unwrap her, and enjoy her. Then they want to make sure that Alex knows about this indiscretion, and then maybe he will be brought back to his senses. They really cannot believe that he really loves her, not at all. And if it is up to them, then they will break him free from this curse, and free him from the pussy-whipping that Sabrina has obviously dished out on him. They really think that they are saving their friend from himself.

Actually, they just want to fuck Sabrina, to find out what secret powers she possesses between her thighs. They are fully aware of Alex's problem, and they cannot believe that tiny Sabrina can take it. They don't have small cocks either, not by a long shot, but none of their meat stands up close to Alex's. They really just need to explore her depths, each of them secretly confident that they can really satisfy her more than Alex can. Surely she must find his abnormally large sausage uncomfortable. Surely she is just in it for the money and the lifestyle and every other perk that comes with being Mrs. Ramsey!

They make a few calls and get some women in the apartment. They need to empty their sacks before returning home to their lives that are about as exciting as parking lots. They all find a corner of the apartment to fuck in, and after they get their rocks off, they dismiss the women. Then they leave, going to their individual homes, thoughts of how and where they can get Sabrina alone uppermost on their minds. This has really become a pastime for all of them, even though not so much for Tom.

Tom looks at his phone in his study, and he thinks that maybe, just maybe he should get a hold of Alex and tell him what is going on. He thinks better of it, though, not wanting to burn himself in the process. A bottle of whiskey suddenly appeals to him, and he opens it. After pouring himself a drink, he starts to let his mind wander to Sabrina again. He locks himself in his study now and turns on his laptop. He goes to a secret folder, one that contains adult videos and images. This is a secret addiction, one that he has managed to keep under control for the longest time.

He positions himself on his large leatherback, pulling on the earphone. He searches for relevant content, under the interracial banner, and he opens the first video. Tom tries to find a woman that looks like Sabrina, but this is not possible. Eventually, he just releases his dick from his trousers, reaches into the drawer for some lubrication, and he starts to beat his own meat. He looks at the surface of the table, and when he spots the tissues, he pulls them a little closer. Then he relaxes into his masturbation session.

Tom cums after a short while, but he continues to watch the video for a while longer. A couple of minutes later he takes a sip of his drink and then cleans up the mess that he made. Afterwards, he packs everything away and goes to the shower. He knows that he will sleep now, but he also knows that he too will not be happy until he has had the pleasure of digging his cock between Sabrina's thighs. He admits to himself that he really wants her, but he also admits to himself that it is for reasons other than just the physical.

Tom has also seen what Alex saw in Sabrina initially. He has seen the fire and drive in her, and this has drawn him to her, more than even her physical appearance has. She is vulnerable, strangely so, even through her new feistiness. Her laugh is like a million effervescent bubbles bursting in a symphony of song. The way she throws her head back too, revealing a long neck the just invites your mouth onto it, is mesmerizing. There are just so many things about her that are just plain down attractive.

He sits alone in his study, thinking about Alex and Sabrina's relationship. He remembers what Alex said to him after his first meeting with Sabrina, the vivid descriptions he gave of her appearance and the wonderfully descriptive way he spoke of her character. Initially, he thought that his friend was exaggerating, but then he met her, and he knew that if anything, Alex's descriptions of this young woman were gross understatements. He wonders if he can have Sabrina, really have her, the way Alex has her.

What could he possibly offer her that would make her leave Alex and come running into his arms?

No amount of money will get Sabrina to leave Alex. Tom knows this. Money is just a by-product, and added bonus for being with Alex. It is not important to Sabrina, and this is obvious too. Tom also knows that he cannot compete with Alex in the bedroom. Besides Alex's huge cock, he knows that Alex pays careful attention to his sexual partners, something that he has not yet been able to master. And of course, there is the little matter of his marriage. If only he had waited before, he put a ring on it.

One way that he could get Sabrina's attention though is if Alex were to cheat. If he could even create the illusion of an affair, then Sabrina might be forced to come to him for comfort, or advice. That would give him a definite advantage over Alex. He pulls out his phone and starts to scroll down the names on it. He wonders which one of his personal side-dishes would be willing to pretend to be having an affair with Alex Ramsey. For the right price, though, he suspects that he could convince anyone of them.

He thinks, though that the best thing would be for him to get someone unknown, to him or Alex. At least this way there would be no way for Alex to link it back to him. He just needs to make sure that it is a very beautiful black girl, one that appeals to Alex's knight-in-shining-armor sensibilities. He looks up the number of a few houses that service the elite of society. A quick internet search reveals about 12 houses that have pictures of their escorts on their websites. Some of them are masked as dating services, but Tom knows better. He also knows that Alex will not ever visit such establishments.

After making a few calls, he has set up three appointments over the next three days. He will need the whole night to convince each girl of the benefits to her of playing this role. He plans a fake business trip so that he doesn't have to explain anything to his wife. After everything is set up, he goes to bed to plan the rest of his trip in his head. He fucks his wife for four minutes, just to appease her, never one to ignore his duties.

He sends his wife a text the next day, informing her of his trip. Then he gets home to find his bag packed already, and his wife waiting to say goodbye to him. He has said that he will be going to Chicago, but he is actually headed to a downtown hotel which will be his home for a few days. He takes enough cash with him so as not to leave a credit card trail. There can be no mistakes now. He needs to do this right or risk failure.

On his way to the hotel, he thinks about what he is doing. He wonders if he should tell Greg and Fred about his plan, but he thinks better of it. He cannot involve these wildcards in this scheme, which, if it is going to work, will require a measure of discretion that is impossible for the other two men who are not known for being subtle. Tom will do this on his own, and when he succeeds at it, then he might let the others in on his little plan. He arrives at the hotel shortly after 6 PM, his first escort due to arrive at around 8.

He has a shower and orders room service. He raids the minibar and then orders another bottle of whiskey, a mixer and a bottle of champagne. He needs to be sure that he plays this right, and that he gets through to at least one of the girls. If not, then, at least, he will have some decent sex and go on his merry way, back to the drawing board. He must get them to cooperate, though, and he wonders how much this cooperation will cost him. Whatever the price, though, he can only hope that it will be worth it.

When the first girl arrives, she is even more beautiful than her pictures. She looks very much like Sabrina, and so Tom cannot hide his excitement. His dick is so hard so quickly that it pitches a massive tent in his pants. She looks down at his cock, and then up at his face, smiling at the effect that she has on this man. Strangely, she is instantly proud of herself, and she starts to plan out in her head how she will please this man who is obviously very excited to see her.

12

Tom pours her a glass of champagne and watches her reactions to it, her movements. Her voice is raspy and sexy, but Tom isn't sure if this is put on for his benefit or if her voice is just naturally textured this way. He speaks to her in one-word sentences, wanting her to do most of the talking, just so that he can listen to her. He also has no way of keeping his erection in his pants too now, because it really just wants to literally burst out of his pants now.

He unzips his pants as she sips on her bubbles. She finishes the contents of the glass and then gets up. She helps him with his belt and then out of his pants. Her name is Mia, and she loves the sound of her name as it comes off his lips. He almost whispers it, and this excites her somewhat, more so than she has ever been excited by any other john. She is sure that she will enjoy this session more so than she has for a number of months. She gets up to her feet and takes his dick in one hand while taking off his shirt with the other hand. Her pussy is now warm and wet.

When she has him completely naked and seated on the couch, she takes off her own dress. She has no underwear on, her youth making this unnecessary. She takes a hand to her pussy and rubs her fingers over the shaven surface, exposing her large clit and her almost extended lips. Tom looks at her cunt with interest, and he rubs his own dick, curiosity feeding his erection all the more. When she moves her fingers to her breasts and starts to sway her hips from side to side as she walks towards him, he holds his dick up, lifting it off his thigh.

Mia sways her hips a little more and then gyrates them in circles to music that isn't playing. She gets to him and places her hands on his knees as she lowers herself to the floor. She runs her fingers up and down his thighs and then takes his balls between her fingers. Mia then works her fingers up his shaft and takes the thick hardness into her mouth. She works her mouth down his shaft, and he is thrilled by the feeling of her mouth on him.

She sucks on his dick slowly, while taking a finger into her pussy. She fingers herself as gently as she is sucking on his cock, and the feeling of his meat in her mouth feeds her fingering. She comes closer and closer to orgasm that she wishes that she can bring him to one at the same time, but this is not possible. She is going to blow first, no matter how hard she tries not to. When she cums the finger inside her slips a little further into her pussy. She touches her deep inside herself.

Mia now holds his dick with both hands and works her mouth harder on his meat. She sucks on the head, licking it and almost biting into it. Then she bites into his shaft, and gently sucks on the places that she just bit into. Then she licks up and down the surface of his cock and sends immense amounts of pleasure into the depths of his cock. He starts to thrust into her mouth, needing to cum too. He goes deeper and deeper into her mouth, finding the back of her throat, rendering her breathless.

After a moment of deep-throating, he cums at last and fills the inside of her mouth with semen. She looks shocked by this, and holds the semen in her mouth, trying to find somewhere to deposit it. There is nothing nearby, and so she takes the glass and spits the contents of her mouth into it. Tom looks disappointed, but he hides it well. He pulls on his cock, resurrecting his erection almost immediately as she pours champagne for herself in the clean glass on the tray. Tom looks at his semen in the other glass and almost giggles at the sight.

After she rinses her mouth with champagne Tom pulls her to him, after putting the glass with his cum in it behind the ice bucket. He pulls her down on the couch and takes her breasts into his mouth. He closes his eyes and calls to mind the woman that he really wishes was here. He hopes that this will feel at least in part as good as the real thing will feel like when he finally gets a chance to bed

Sabrina. For now, though, this whore will have to do the trick.

He sucks on her tits for a long while before working his mouth up to her neck. He knows that whores have a rule about kissing, so he doesn't even try for her mouth. She comes to him with hers, though, so that he knows that this rule will be forgone for tonight at least. They kiss, and he sucks the taste of licorice and champagne off her tongue. He sends his tongue deep into her mouth and then plays with the tops of all her teeth. Then he plays with her tongue for a while before driving his tongue deeper into her mouth.

Then he is on her neck again, and then on her breasts. He works his way down her belly, and when he finally settles on her clit, she wraps her legs around his neck. She pulls him hard onto her pussy, and he sucks on it hard. Then he sends his tongue into her pussy and pulls the taste out of her cunt. He sucks on her pussy long and hard, until his dick starts to ache, wanting to be inside her now. He begins to think about where he put the condoms, and when he finally remembers, he relaxes into the extreme muff-dive that he is giving Mia.

He sucks on her a moment longer, and then just before she cum he pulls his mouth off her. She shakes, trying to pull him back onto her cunt, but he has a strong neck, and so he pulls her legs apart with his head. Then he looks at her shuddering, enjoying that he is responsible for this. He has never been with a black woman like this before, and so he really enjoys the taste of her. It is different, primal almost, and he cannot hide the fact that he really likes this.

Tom gets up to his feet, and he brings Mia with him. He leads her to the bed and picks up the condoms from his pocket on the way. By the time they get to the bed, he has wrapped his cock carefully in the plastic, lubricated sheath. He follows her down onto the bed, parting her legs with his body, sending himself into her. She feels every bit as food as he imagines that she would, but he is still less than satisfied with her, knowing in the back of his mind that he would rather be with Sabrina.

The woman that he has now,

though, the woman that he is practically impaling with his dick, is no less attractive, though. After thrusting into her a few times he finally gets into it, and he is suddenly here in this room with her. He fucks her for the longest time, enjoying it thoroughly, and working himself up to climax. By the time he has an exhausted orgasm, he has brought her to three. He lies there with his dick inside her for a while longer, and then he pulls out and sorts out the condom.

He walks around the room naked, watching Mia lying on the bed, gathering herself. There is a moment when he feels like he should just come out with his request, but he knows that there are a few things that he has to get clear in his head first. He pours them both a drink, and he goes to join her on the bed. She knows not to ask too many questions, johns usually not wanting to talk, or if they do, they like to be the ones initiating the conversation. They just lie there drinking, Tom thinking about how best to approach his request.

Tom wonders though why he is so worried about this. Surely it is just a financial transaction. What if though, Alex counter-offers? If he got wind of this plan, and if he met Mia, really met her, and then surely he would counter the offer that he makes to her. He starts to throw figures around in his head, thinking what would be acceptable to this whore, and what would be considered an insult. He is suddenly very confused, and Mia, reading this confusion that she knows nothing about, decides to do the only thing that she can think of.

She takes his cock into her mouth and sucks the softness hard again. She takes her tongue and swirls it around the head, and then works her mouth down on the shaft again. She nibbles into the flesh that forms the hard trunk of his tool now and then pulls her mouth off of it briefly. Then she hides his cock in her mouth again and sucks on it very hard. Swirling her tongue around his head again brings him back into the moment, removing from his mind everything that was moments earlier floating around in there.

He watches Mia working on his tool, and he enjoys what he sees. She moves her mouth over the full surface of the shaft, while holding it upright, and watching his reactions to the oral action that he is getting. He keeps on closing his eyes, but then he opens them again, wanting to watch her work. He sips on his drink again and then realizes that he has emptied the glass completely. He drops the glass on the bed and takes his fingers to her hair. He moves the tips of his fingers over her head, wanting to push her down on his dick, but not.

Tom starts to writhe under her mouth now, bending and straightening his legs as he gets closer and closer to orgasm. When he eventually shoots into her mouth, she swallows this time, and he smiles to himself. He has completely forgotten the moment earlier when she spat his seed repulsively from her mouth into the champagne glass. He holds her head down in his cock now and thrusts gently up and into her mouth. Tom makes sure that his dick has completely been emptied now before he allows her to lift herself off him.

Then he pulls her up so that they lie side by side. He watches her face, looking for something in her that says that she will be able to pull this request off. He thinks he sees it, and then he gets up to refill their glasses. There is something about drinking that actually seems to calm him down, her too. He figures that it is now or never, and if she is going to agree or not to what he has to ask her, she just needs to know. He takes a deep breath.

"How do you feel about roleplaying?" he asks her, testing the waters.

"I love roleplaying," she replies, not really understanding the question.

"And what would you say if I asked you to role-play with another man?" he tests further.

"You mean like a threesome?" she asks, proving that she really doesn't get what she is being asked. Tom laughs, downing the remainder of his drink. He looks at her and shakes his head, both in disbelief and in response to what she is asking him. He searches his head for another way to ask her what he really wants to know now.

Tom decides to wait a bit before posing the question again. He is hard again, and his cock needs some attention. He pulls her onto him with her mouth again and watches himself disappearing into her face. He lips wrap snuggly around his meat, and he pulls her up and down on himself, watching her eagerly eat his dick. She really is good at this, which makes this a more than pleasant interview. He comes close to cumming and just before he busts a nut he pulls her off his dick.

He lays her flat on her back again, and observes her breasts heaving, and her pussy arching up towards him. He knows she wants him to fuck her again, and he will oblige. He mounts her, and enters her aching cunt, enjoying the way it seems to be beating against his cock. Tom fucks her deliciously slowly now, concentrating on each thrust, going into her all the way, and pulling his cock almost all the way out. He enjoys the moans that he draws from her on each insertion, enjoys the way she bites her bottom lip every time his cock hits the back of her pussy.

Before he cums, he pulls himself out of her completely. Tom turns her over and brings her to her knees. He places his cock between her cheeks and teases her asshole. He doesn't expect it to give way so easily, but it does. She is apparently used to being fucked up the ass. He watches as his cock slips easily into this hole, and the excitement inside him grows immensely. He pushes himself into her, all the way, and she moans softly. She enjoys this, apparently. He starts to thrust into her ass, parting her cheeks with both hands so that he can have a clear view of this achievement.

She literally feeds him her ass, pushing into each of his thrusts. He stops moving and watches her work her ass around his thickness. She gyrates her ass around his cock and then pulls away a little bit. Then she pushes back on him, taking all of him into her hole again. Mia works her ass around his thickness so expertly that he doesn't need to do anything. He just stays propped up on his knees and watches her bring him to a spectacular climax. After he cums too she doesn't stop, milking every last drop from his cock, which is still remarkably hard.

He feels like he owes her for this pleasure. So he pulls his cock from her ass slowly and pushes her down on the bed. Then he sends his softening dick into her cunt from her back. She parts her legs and tries to wrap her legs around him, which is impossible, though, in her current position. She just has to lie there, and take him into her, enjoying his thickening cock again. For his age, Tom is quite virile. Mia loves it. She knew that she would enjoy this man. She just didn't know how much she would enjoy him.

Tom fucks her slowly again, needing to relax his cock a bit, but happy that it is as solid as ever, able to reach deep into her. He drives himself into her repeatedly, and she hides her face in the pillows, screaming into them at the pleasure that is being delivered into her with each massive thrust. He almost lifts her up off the bed with his cock now, and she comes with him with each scoop. There is something primal about the way he is fucking her now, and this drives her absolutely insane.

He brings her to another orgasm, and then another, and then he brings himself to a final climax, completely exhausted. He stays inside her, though, leaning into her ear. He whispers his request to her, and she doesn't hear him at first. Then his request settles over her like a table cloth, and she finally understands what she is being asked. Mia doesn't respond for a moment so that Tom repeats his request. Then she grinds her pussy on him from underneath him; his erection lost completely now, but the full length of his cock still inside her.

"How much..." she asks him eventually.

"Well, if you do a good job, make it believable...ten thousand..." Tom says, throwing a ballpark figure out there, not sure if it is excessive, or if perhaps it will be seen as too little.

She manages to pull her pussy free from him, and then after he lifts himself off her, she turns around to face him. She looks him in his eyes, checking to see if he is serious. He is, and he looks at her for an answer. She smiles, confirming that she is in. He almost kisses her, but then he remembers the rule with whores. He just rolls over and closes his eyes, letting his mind drift to this plan that he has. He falls asleep, knowing that he has lined up his first ally. Two more, and he will be good to go.

When he gets up the next morning, Mia has left. She has left him a note too, with her direct number on it, and three Xs. He smiles at himself, knowing that he has hooked her. Maybe it was the ten thousand; maybe it's just the excitement of his proposition. Whatever it is, at least, he knows that he has one in the bag. He pulls out his laptop, and after ordering breakfast, he scrolls down the list of escorts on a popular site. He chooses a few more and arranges for a few more meetings over the next couple of days.

The girls come to his hotel room, one at a time. He fucks them first and then lays out his proposition. Some of them don't agree with him, some of them try to get more money. But by the end of his 'business trip', he has three perfect little kittens, willing to do his bidding. All he has to do now is set this game into play, and watch Alex and Sabrina come undone. Then he will position himself perfectly to be Sabrina's shoulder to cry on. Then he will get a taste of her, a real taste, and his appetite will be satisfied.

Alex and Sabrina are oblivious to this plan. Sabrina though is still troubled by what happened in the Caymans, thinking of whether or not she should just come out and tell Alex. Alex is aware of what is going on, though, certainly not a stupid man, and he just waits for her to come to him. He is patient, but he is not so patient as to watch what is his at last slip through his fingers. He thinks of telling his friends to back off. But something in him wants to see how Sabrina is going to play this.

Greg, Fred, and Tom come over to his penthouse for drinks one evening. They all seem a little nervous, a little edgy so that Alex has to ask them what's up. They make up various excuses, but he knows what is really going on here. They want to see Sabrina, want to feed their individual fantasies. But she is nowhere to be seen, hiding herself from these perverts in their bedroom. After all, this seems to be a boys' night, and she gives Alex the freedom he needs to be one of the boys.

Tom needs to get his plan into action, and for this to happen, he needs to get Alex out of his apartment. He suggests that they go out for a drink, to a pub that they frequented in their single days. Alex checks with Sabrina, and when he finds her asleep, he decides to go, after leaving her a note of course. They head out, and Tom waits for the perfect moment to set in motion a carefully orchestrated sequence of events. He has to get this just right for it to work, and he intends to do just that.

He goes to the bathroom at the pub and makes a phone call. Mia has to get this right too, and she has to get this right tonight. Then he joins the others again, and orders a round of drinks, waiting for the young woman to make an appearance. It takes her an hour to get there, and by this time, Alex is quite drunk. The timing of it couldn't have been more perfect, and Mia couldn't have been better prepared for this role if she tried. She looks every bit like Sabrina, even sounding like her, almost.

There is something that she has got just perfect about the look that Tom even thinks that she is Sabrina for a moment. But then he takes a closer look at her and realizes that she is, in fact, the girl that he is going to pay to play a very specific role. She walks past them, and then lingers in the background, getting all of their attention. Then she disappears into the crowd for a moment and then makes a re-appearance. Alex is more than a little caught up with this woman, and Tom watches him carefully.

Alex gets up and goes after this woman who looks so much like his wife. He knows in the back of his head that it couldn't possibly be her, but he has to check. He follows her to the bathrooms and watches her walk into the male bathroom. He follows her inside, and when he gets into the room, she is suddenly nowhere to be seen. He checks the cubicles, one at a time, and when he gets to the third one, she suddenly pops out. Alex takes a closer look at her and realizes that it is not Sabrina. He apologizes and turns to leave.

Mia pulls him into the cubicle with her, and he stumbles. He almost falls into the cubicle, landing with both hands on the sides of the toilet. He recovers nicely, though, not sure why he is feeling as light-headed as he is. He can usually handle his alcohol, but now he is feeling more than a little dizzy. He apologizes again and gets to his feet. He tries to push past the woman now standing against the door. She refuses to let him go, undoing his pants and whipping out his cock. He tries to push her off him, but before he can, she has her mouth on him already, trying as best as she can to get his thickness into her mouth.

He knows that this isn't his wife's mouth, though, so he pushes her off of him. But too late, she lets him go. Tom has managed to get a picture of them in a very compromising position, and he gets out of the bathroom. He puts his phone in his pocket and leaves Alex to sort out this messy moment. Alex rejoins them shortly, and after calling a cab, he leaves them suddenly. All of the other men wonder where the hell he ran off too, but they return to their drinks, and Tom raises his glass to Mia as she disappears once and for all into the crowd.

There is much more in store for Alex though, and he is ready to elevate this game to the next level. He knows somehow that a picture of another woman's mouth on her man might not be enough for Sabrina to leave him; it might not be enough for her to run to Tom for comfort. He needs to get the other women into the game, and he needs to, if possible, get Alex to be in bed with one of these women, all of them maybe. He looks at the other two guys, thinking if he should maybe tell them about his plan. But then he thinks better of it, thinking of how he can position himself as Sabrina's go-to-guy when she finds out about Alex's infidelity.

13

Alex gets home a little more sober than he just was. He goes into the shower to wash the recent encounter off himself, feeling strangely dirty and surprisingly aroused. When he gets back into the bedroom, he finds Sabrina awake, sitting up. He is still busy drying himself, still completely naked, still dripping.

"You have a good time?" she asks him, really wanting to know.

"It was alright, except for the woman who followed me to the bathroom and put my dick in her mouth..." he watches her face, looking for a response.

"Seriously?" she asks him, not sure if he is joking or not.

"Seriously...it was very strange..." he responds, waiting for her to blow up.

"And how did you respond?" she presses, not sure though how a woman could get her man with his pants down and get so far as to put his dick in her mouth.

"I pushed her off me and got out of there..." he says, finishing on his back and jumping into bed still naked. "There is just one mouth that I want on me..." he says, noticing that she has seen the humor in this situation, even though she obviously doesn't understand what went down in the club, not entirely.

Sabrina bends over to Alex's side of the bed and starts to swallow his cock. It hardens almost immediately so that she knows that he definitely hasn't had a recent orgasm. Maybe some random woman did put his cock in her mouth, and maybe she did suck on it briefly. But he obviously managed to pull himself free from her, and she is impressed because she knows that he was more than a little drunk, and she knows that he had no reason, besides her of course, to stop himself from letting his meat be eaten.

She shows her appreciation by taking as much of it into her mouth as possible. She works every part of her mouth on every part of his dick, and even the parts that are not in her mouth are paid attention to. Sabrina nibbles up and down the shaft, licking it like she would an ice-cream cone or an ice-lolly, and then she sinks her teeth into the firm flesh again. When she gets down to his balls, sucking, licking and then biting, he almost pulls away. He doesn't though, enjoying the feeling immensely.

Sabrina sucks on his balls for the longest time, really enjoying the taste of freshly showered on him. He starts to sweat, though, and she enjoys the salty taste too. She knows that he is drunk, but not so drunk now not to want to fuck her. She is wet between her thighs now, wanting him to fuck her. But she is patient, and she has had enough sleep for her not to be tired. If Alex can handle this session, then so can she. She needs to make sure that he doesn't regret, ever, marrying her, and promising her happily ever after.

She goes to work on his head now, thick, swollen, and dripping with pre-cum. She licks it and sucks on it, and he cannot help but thrust into her mouth now. She sucks harder and harder on it, edging him over to victory. He doesn't even try to hold himself back, fucking her mouth harder now, driving his dick deeper and deeper into her mouth. She wraps her mouth tightly around the first few inches of his dick now as he thrusts into her with real verve, almost at the end. She knows that he is going to blow at any moment now, and she braces herself for this eruption.

When he cums, he shoots a steady stream of semen straight into the back of her throat. She starts to swallow almost immediately, not wanting to waste a single drop. Alex closes his eyes and holds her head in place, tightly. She lets him move her head over his cock, her mouth still tight around the shaft, concentrating on the never-ending seed that is literally pouring out of his cock. When he stops cumming, she swallows the remainder of the lava, and eventually pulls her mouth off his cock.

She must rinse her mouth, the feeling of sticky goo prominent on her teeth. Her tongue too is riddled with the taste of her man, and she likes it. She wants to kiss him, though, and she is never sure how he feels about tasting himself in her mouth. When she comes out of the bathroom, she looks directly at him, smiling, holding a glass of champagne out to her. She cannot think when he had the time to go downstairs and get it, but she appreciates it nonetheless.

They sip on the bubbles for a moment before Alex is settling into the space between her legs. He immediately goes for her clit with his teeth, biting harder then he intended so that she lets out a soft scream. He apologizes, and goes for the same spot with his lips and then his tongue, feeding his apology onto her pussy now, with his mouth. Then he snakes into her pussy with his tongue, and she holds his head tightly. She literally pulls him into her, as she takes his tongue deeper and deeper into her pussy.

He eats her out expertly. She cums hard twice before he finally removes his head from between her legs. He traces additional kisses up her belly and French-kisses her naval. Then he lands on her breasts with his mouth and takes them one at a time into him, his tongue working miracles on her nipples. Then he bites into her nipples with his teeth, gently this time, and sends shards of intense pleasure into her entire breast, and then into her chest. He bites a little harder, and the pleasure makes its way to her pussy. She wraps her legs around him now.

Alex finds her holes quickly and plugs it completely with his massive rod. He starts to ease his way inside her, and finds her tight, but willing. Her pussy seems to shrink at the thought of him, but he knows this by now. He is aware of the workings of her tiny frame and nudges on, gently. Soon half of his dick is inside her, and she is breathing deeply. She is used to him by now, but still it is a massive adjustment. She doesn't even need to tell him that she is okay anymore. She knows that if she has to say it, then he probably won't believe her.

He goes deeper into her, and she starts to moan her deep sensual moans. He has really mastered the art of fucking her, despite his huge fucking cock. He goes into her slowly, and then with a little more intensity, just to surprise her. Then he slows down, easing part of his cock out of her before her goes in as deep as he can. He repeats this trick, warming her pussy up immensely. She starts to sweat from deep inside, and then she is taking him so far into the back of her cunt that he feels that he is all the way up inside her.

She has a massive orgasm, contained and subdued, but extremely explosive at the same time. Sabrina cannot breathe, but still she moans loudly. As he eases his cock out of her, she knows that he hasn't cum yet. The alcohol seems to be keeping his orgasm at bay. She doesn't want him to fall asleep without cumming, though. She has made a secret pact with herself that never will she let their sex-life end with one of them not completely satisfied. Alex is tired, though, and she knows this. Thought comes to her suddenly, and she braces herself as she turns him onto his back.

She goes for his cock with her mouth again, licking every trace of her orgasm off his meat. She never thought that she would like this, but now she does. Sabrina is hooked on the taste of herself, especially and only off of Alex though. She knows that she probably will not be with another man for the rest of her life, or his. But that is not a thought that she wants to entertain right now.

Alex is still hard, very hard. His dick is so thick, so fat though and so incredibly long that it just lies to the side of his naval. She sandwiches his cock between his belly and her pussy and starts to grind. He looks at her with a question mark in his eyes, not sure if she is actually about to do what he thinks she is. Then she raises herself off his cock enough for her to point it directly at her hole. She smiles, takes a deep breath, and the slips the first few inches of him inside herself.

She holds herself up by placing both her hands on his belly. She also goes up so that she is holding herself up basically at her toes. Then she starts to slowly, very slowly, work his cock into her tight pussy, appreciating that it is still wet from her recent orgasm. Sabrina doesn't look at her cunt now, trusting her feelings more than her sight. She also doesn't want to see the damage being done to her. She has no intention of impaling herself on Alex, but she knows that this is a very clear and very present risk.

When he hits the back of her cunt, as deep as he is possibly going to go, she stops. She is on her knees now but still has her cunt hovering carefully above and on Alex's throbbing python. His dick pulsates so sporadically that she feels these pulses in her belly. She knows that he is as nervous as she is, but she also knows that he is very excited by this. She never takes the initiative this way, not with the size of Alex's tool, and he really likes this side of her, appreciating the effort.

She lifts off of his cock slightly, and then sinks herself back down on it so that he is lodged firmly inside her again. Again she raises herself off him somewhat, determined to find her rhythm. When she does, Alex smiles, and she knows that she is doing it right. She starts to ride his dick, as hard as she can, but very slowly. Alex closes his eyes and tilts his head back. He reaches for her breasts and takes them both in either one of his hands. He squeezes hard, and she rides him even harder. There is a definite rhythm, a succinct flow to what is now happening not only to Alex's cock but also to her cunt.

He opens his eyes a few times, to make sure that he isn't dreaming. He watches her moving on him, watches his fingers over her breasts. He moves his hands down to her waist and then rests his fingers on her thighs. There is no need for him to move her over him, to control her. She seems to have this entire escapade covered. Then he closes his eyes again and just relaxes into the enjoyment of what is happening to him. It is absolutely beautiful. He mouths 'I love you' to her so many times, every syllable resting on her ears lightly so that she knows that she hears it but still feels like she is dreaming.

She keeps on riding him, trying to bring him to climax. Instead, she has another orgasm, and she wets his cock, dropping her lower onto his cock, making her feel very uncomfortable but not so uncomfortable that she pulls herself free of his cock. Instead, after a moment, after she has caught her breath, she resumes her grinding. She has caught her footing now, and she really works her pussy on every inch of his dick inside her, bringing him closer and closer to his own orgasm.

Alex breathes deep, and he starts to thrust up into her involuntarily. He really cannot help himself now, so close is he to orgasm. She braces herself against his trusting and lifts herself slightly above her man, to give him room to thrust without slicing clear through her with his cock. It seems to be growing thicker with every stroke, and she finds her mouth opening wider and wider, almost as though he were fucking her in this space and not her pussy. Her hands have started to slip over his belly now too, and onto his chest, because of the sweat that falls from him in large beads now.

She is holding his neck now, her lips on him, as her cunt takes some considerable beating. There still no sign of orgasm on Alex's part, even though she is on a clear path towards another one. She really loves him, madly. Not even just because he fucks her so well, but it is certainly a big part of it. Her pussy falls on his cock now as he tries and fails to go deeper. There really just is no more space inside her for him. He is just too damn big. But she is glad that she has at least adjusted to him so much that he knows how far he can stretch her, fully aware of her limits.

Sabrina holds tighter onto his neck, not kissing him anymore, just breathing into his mouth and over his face. She tightens her grip with her thighs around his waist, trying to control to whatever extent she can the amount of his dick that is moving into her. Soon enough though she is having another orgasm and soon enough he is plugging deeper into her than ever before and she almost screams. She kisses him again, trying to silence herself, knowing that if he even gets a hint that she is uncomfortable, he will stop, before he has had a chance to relieve himself. She will not have that.

Alex goes into her with renewed energy now, and she pushed down on him, meeting him halfway. She holds herself tighter to him, hoping that he will cum soon, knowing though that this isn't likely. He sends his arms around her back now, holding her in place. Again he cannot help himself, thrusting into her harder and harder. She stops moving her pussy altogether now, just letting him do what he needs to. She is enjoying it, though, but she is starting to feel him in the pit of her stomach so that she feels that he could at any moment pierce right through her pussy into the pit of her belly. Sabrina just squeezes her cunt as tight as she can over his tool, edging him closer and closer to the edge.

When he finally blows, he screams. He shouts out loud, catching her by total surprise so that she has to look at him to make sure that he is okay. There are few things as erotic as this, and as he has a massive orgasm she feels the beginnings of yet another one. He keeps on thrusting into her, reading her body perfectly. Soon enough she is cumming too, for the last time, knowing that she couldn't possibly handle another orgasm. She cums hard, and he starts to ease himself out of her, knowing that she needs to really recover from him.

He holds her to him, bringing her down from her orgasm by kissing her lightly on her lips and then on her neck. She knows the she loves her husband, and she trusts him. Thoughts of Fred, Tom and Greg suddenly flood into her mind, and she wonders if she has not been dishonest with him by not telling him what has been happening. After all, he was honest with her about what happened tonight, and she appreciates it. Maybe he will appreciate it if she just lets him know what his friends have been up to. Is it not too late now though?

Sabrina watches him sleep now, her mind racing with all these thoughts. She cannot even sneak out of bed because she is locked in Alex's arms, and he is sleeping so peacefully that she doesn't want to wake him. She thinks about everything that has happened in the last year, with Alex's friends, and without them. She thinks about how her life has changed and where she comes from. She also thinks of Lyle, strangely enough, and she wonders why she never before thought of getting advice from him. Gay men are usually very good at this sort of thing.

She makes a note to call him in the morning and to arrange a lunch. Then she will let him know everything that has been going on and get his take on the problem. She closes her eyes and gets some sleep, needing it more now after her midnight treat. Alex really takes everything out of her, and she enjoys giving it. He deserves every part of her, and not just for everything that he has given her. He deserves everything for the man that he is, good, kind, generous to a fault, and super sexy for his age. He can really give much younger men a run for their money.

They wake up together and start kissing immediately. Alex isn't hard yet, but it doesn't take long for him to be sporting a massive morning glory. He doesn't enter Sabrina immediately, though, wanting to treat her this morning. She is still kissing him as he slips a long, thick finger between her thighs, and then into her snatch. He enters her slowly, and when his finger is all the way inside her he uses his thumb on the same hand to rub gently on her clit. He moves the finger inside her around in the same direction as the circles that he is pressing into her clitoris with his thumb, and her pussy starts to warm.

Alex doesn't add another finger, although he is really tempted. He just begins to ease the one that is already inside her in and out, slowly in, and then very slowly, very gently out. He does this over and over again, wetting her pussy as he goes. She starts to pant softly so that he knows that he is hitting the spot. He doesn't remove his thumb from her clit either, just fingering her ever so slowly with just this one finger.

She starts to gasp now, and then to moan oh so softly. He keeps his pace consistent, in absolutely no hurry to get anywhere. He keeps on fucking her with this finger until she starts to breathe short, shallow breaths and he knows that she is having an orgasm. He keeps kissing her throughout and when she digs her fingers into his back, and then into his neck, he knows that he has got her to just the right place. But he is far from done treating her, gently removing the finger from her pussy, taking his thumb off her clit too as he makes his very graceful exit.

Then he disappears under the covers and parts his wife's legs. He hasn't tasted her, really tasted her, in a minute, and he settles his face snuggly between her thighs. He starts to kiss her cunt, up and down, starting at the base and working his way up to her clit. Then he kisses her pussy lips and sends his tongue out to part them so that he has access to her hole. He starts to French kiss her snatch now, devouring all the flavors that he finds there.

He uses every part of his mouth on every part of her pussy now, and she rewards him with a steady stream of cream from her depths. She wraps her legs around his head, around his neck, and then parts her legs even more. He holds her legs in place now, open wide, and far apart, giving him direct and uncompromised access to her pussy now. He really goes into her cunt now, and Alex really sucks all of the juices flowing from within Sabrina. He sucks her dry, and she just wets herself shortly after again.

After she has had an intense second orgasm, Alex brings her to a third with just his tongue. He inserts it into her pussy deeply and fucks her with his thick, wet, hot, fleshy tongue. She squirts into his mouth now so that he has a spray of cunt-juice in his 5'oclock shadow, on his face, and mostly in his mouth. He licks it off his face, and then he kisses her cunt and clit to say thank you to her. Then he pulls her down so that his cock is positioned above her cunt now, and he kisses her up her belly until he finally settles on her breasts.

Alex makes good on his tongue threats on her nipples, after licking them profusely for the longest time, teasing her cunt with his erection. He sucks on her tits in their entirety now as he starts to make his way into her pussy. When he gets all the way inside her he moves up to her neck and then to her lips, and seals the deal, fucking her gently for a solid two hours until he brings himself, and her, to a grand final orgasm. His virility is impressive, and it seems to be getting better and better with age.

They fuck again in the shower and

have a long, languid breakfast. Then she kisses him and makes her way to the lunch that she has already planned with Lyle. She is itching to tell him the story now, really wanting to hear what he will have to say about this situation. Lyle is gob smacked, but not really surprised, knowing the caliber of men that Sabrina is describing. He just shakes his head and takes another sip of his drink before he asks her about the elephant in the room.

"Have you told Alex?" he asks her.

"No, I didn't want to complicate his relationship with them..." Sabrina answers, realizing now that she has said it out loud how absurd this thinking was.

"And so you decided to risk your relationship with him instead?" Lyle is honest; he cannot help himself. Sabrina appreciates it.

They formulate a strategy going forward. Sabrina has never been the calculating agenda type, but now she has to be. If she is going to save her marriage and herself from further torture, then she is going to have to sacrifice a few of Alex's friendships on the proverbial alter. She reminds herself though that she did nothing wrong, and if this plan that she has come up with along with her only ally in New York, Lyle, then this will become very obvious to all concerned. She air-kisses him and makes her way back to her apartment, to put together her plan, and hoping to god that it works.

Another plan is underway across town too, Tom's plan. He is determined to undermine the trust that Sabrina has in Alex, and to make himself her refuge. He also senses that he is running out of time, and so he has a meeting with his chosen whores, his own group of little helpers, and they are briefed about the next step to his elaborate but not very clever plan. He needs to get Alex naked with just one of them, if not all of them, and he needs to get recorded footage of this liaison. Then he needs to get this footage in Sabrina's hands and be waiting with open arms for her to come running to him, teary eyed and legs wide open. He only hopes that this will give him the access to her pussy that he really wants.

14

Alex is really busy over the next couple of days, so Tom doesn't have an opportunity to get him alone. He decides to make it a group thing and invite them to go sailing, Fred, and Greg too, and the whores he has hired to get Alex into bed. Fred and Greg think that they are gifts for them, and make themselves more than a little comfortable with them.

Sabrina tries to shake the fact that these women look just like her from her head. She wonders if this isn't just their way of showing her that they could have her if they wanted to, albeit versions of her. Still it is a little uncanny, and she is more than a little uncomfortable. She plays it cool, though, thinking that it will just be a quick sailing trip around the harbor, and then they will be back on dry land, and she can remove her man from these clones.

She watches as one of the women comes up to Alex and asks him to help her with her bikini top. Why didn't she ask one of the other men who obviously have no qualms cheating on their wives? Still, Alex is a gentleman, and he helps her. When she turns around and kisses him, thank you it takes everything in Sabrina not to get up and punch her. She gets up and goes down below, to their cabin, to freshen up. If this is the game they want to play, then so be it. Now is as good a time as any to put her own plan into action.

Sabrina wears the kind of bikini that leaves very little to the imagination. When she surfaces again, all eyes are definitely on her, and she makes the other women look like catholic school girls by comparison. Tom is immediately hard so that he pulls his own whore on him to hide his excitement. Sabrina has seen this already, and she decides to turn things up a few serious notches. She takes Alex's face in her hands and kisses him long and deep, and then turns to the bar, and mixes a pitcher of cocktails which she serves to everybody.

She lingers at the other men, letting them look her over, letting them take in the view completely. Then she gets to her husband and kisses him again before handing him his glass. They lie down on a chaise, and she runs her fingers up and down his leg, watching the other men watching her touch her man. Alex is a little surprised by her behavior, but he likes it, he likes this possessive side of her, making him feel that he is the only man that she wants. Essentially, he is.

Sabrina hopes that this works the way she sees it in her mind. She goes for her man's lips again and then excuses herself. She can only hope that one of the men will follow her and that her husband will follow him. There is no other way. She has got to get this trap just right, so that Alex can hear him make advances, hear her reject him, and that will bring everything that has been happening in the light. Sure, the rest of this trip will be more than a little uncomfortable, but so what. She just needs to nip it in the bud once and for all.

Greg is the one who takes the bait. He follows her to the bathroom, and then as she disappears, he holds the door open, looking up and down the hallway, checking that nobody has followed them. When he sees nobody he pushes his way into the small space and looks at Sabrina, up and down, a hunger hanging in his eyes, his mouth already salivating. Sabrina isn't sure if he really wants her for who she is, or if it is just a game that they are playing with her because she belongs to Alex.

"Really Greg, really?" she asks.

"Really... why are you doing this to me...? I really want you!" he lets her know immediately what his intentions are.

"Well, you can never have me. I'm Alex's wife, and whether or not you respect that, or whether or not you respect me is actually irrelevant... But you will respect my husband. Now get out!" she speaks loudly, emphatically. She doesn't know if Alex has heard this, but he has, and he turns and high-tails it out of the hallway before Greg makes an appearance. Yes, he tested Sabrina, and yes he let her be subjected to the most terrible treatment at the hands of his friends. But he just had to be sure, and he is. He is more that sure, in fact.

Greg is the first one to come back up on the deck. He looks a little flustered, and Alex knows just why. He keeps an eye out for Sabrina, but she doesn't seem to be making an appearance. He gets up to go and check on her, but another woman hijacks him, asking him to rub a little sunscreen on her back. She will obviously not take no for an answer, and again Alex wonders why she doesn't ask one of the men that she was obviously brought for to do it. After letting out a huge sigh, he takes the bottle of sunscreen and rubs it on her back, all the while looking out for his wife.

He is nervous, more than he should be, but he trusts that Sabrina can see what is going on here. When he is finished with the woman's back he gets up and starts to make his way to the stairs that will lead him down below. Tom stops him this time, instructing him to fill their glasses with champagne. Alex obliges, although he isn't even sure why. This is certainly not the kind of party for a married couple to be at, and certainly not together. He passes the flutes around, very aware that all the women on the yacht's beautiful deck are looking at him, at his chest, and particularly at his crotch.

There is something strangely familiar about Mia too, although he doesn't know her name. She has also been introduced to him as somebody else, but he doesn't know this. The last time he saw her they exchanged no pleasantries, his focus was on getting his dick into her mouth. Alex doesn't remember this, not really, just having a distinct sense of déjà vu every time he passes her. Still Sabrina is conspicuously absent from the deck, and he starts to really worry about her.

Fred has his whore pulled close to him now, and he is running her fingers up and down the length · of his obviously erect cock. This is going to be that kind of party, Alex senses, and he wishes suddenly that he and his wife had declined this invitation. There is no turning back now, though, nowhere to go, so they will just have to ride it out. When Fred removes his cock from his shorts and settles the woman's mouth on it, Alex is suddenly relieved that Sabrina isn't on deck to see this shit.

Tom and Greg watch this action, also getting more than a little hard. Alex too starts to sport and erection, involuntarily of course, and he turns into the bar to make some much-needed adjustments to his trousers. Greg pulls his shorts off completely and goes to lie down on the chaise next to Fred, encouraging the woman sucking Fred's dick to give him a little attention too. She does, totally oblivious to anything and anyone around them.

Alex really starts to panic now, Tom seeing this. Tom takes another pitcher of drinks from the bar and smiles at Alex, shaking his head, in seeming disapproval. But this is exactly what he had hoped would happen. He turns away from Alex and slips something into the pitcher, powdered ecstasy, knowing the effect that this has always had on Alex and his morality, and also his inhibitions. He passes glasses around the room, and everyone except the cocksucker takes a glass, emptying its contents quickly down their throats. Tom doesn't drink, though, pretending to, and he watches as Alex drains his own glass down.

He hands Alex another glass, on the premise that he is just trying to relax him. He asks where Sabrina disappeared to, reminding Alex that he is minus his wife. Alex has no answer for his friend, emptying this second glass of ecstasy-laced cocktail down his throat. It starts to take effect rather quickly, and the deck very soon turns into a party. Mia comes up to Alex and takes his mammoth cock between her fingers. He pulls away from her and walks over to the furthest chair on the deck, needing to create some distance between himself and this woman he suddenly remembers.

Mia doesn't take this as rejection. Instead, on Tom's non-verbal instruction, she follows Alex to the chair, and as soon as he lies down, she straddles him, pulling his dick from his shorts in one swift move. Alex tries in vain to get her off him, the ecstasy dancing on every part of his skin now, making him incredibly horny. His dick goes hard, and Mia runs her fingers up and down the impressive shaft. Tom starts to tap on the bar, anxious, wanting Sabrina to come out now. She does too and looks around for her husband.

Spotting him in the corner with his cock in another woman's hands she goes white. She steps back, but not before Tom has seen her. She turns back into the hallway and marches towards her room. She does this just before she can see Alex finally succeed at getting Mia off him. Tom sees an opportunity, though, and he follows Sabrina quickly to the room. It's now or never; he thinks, and he follows her to the still-open door. He closes it behind himself, and then locks it.

Sabrina looks up, not crying but wanting too. He comes in close to her and pulls her to him, embracing her, a mock gesture of sympathy. She knows better, though, and she pushes him away, revealing his already exposed penis. It is a long dick too, but not as long as her husband. It is long enough to graze her belly button though as

Tom staggers back towards the door. She looks at his cock for a moment and then moves her eyes to his face.

"What the fuck are you doing?" she asks him.

"What do you think?" he asks back, stroking his hardness.

"Get the hell out of here..." she says, almost begging him.

"Is that what you really want?" Tom presses, settling the tip of his index finger in the eye of his snake.

"Yes," she responds, making her way around him and unlocking the door. She pulls it open just as Alex appears in the doorway, and then stumbling into the room. He sees Tom in the space, but Tom turns before he can see his exposed manhood. He hurries to get it back in his pants, asking Alex if he's okay, suggesting to Sabrina that maybe he needs to lie down. Sabrina helps her man to the bed, seeing that something is different with him. She knows immediately that someone must have spiked his drink.

Why wouldn't they too, she thinks. She sends Tom out of the room with her eyes, and she helps Alex to bed. Alex isn't about to sleep, but he is very frustrated by how he feels. This was the reason he stopped taking recreational drugs in the first place, this lack of control over himself. He lays back, trying to gather himself, attempting to figure out what happened. Fuck Tom, he thinks, remembering the pitcher that he poured from. Alex laughs, though, knowing that this is not how Tom saw this playing out.

He pulls Sabrina close to him and whispers his condition in her ear. She laughs too, not sure what he is going through but from what she sees she knows that she just needs to be here for him until the effect of the drug wears off. Shit, these guys will stop at nothing. There must be a way to get them to back off once and for all, though, and the gears start to turn in Sabrina's head. There is movement in Alex's head too, although for largely different reasons. He is proud of himself, though. He really is every bit a married man. He knows this, and he feels it with every fiber of his being.

This sinister plot is very obvious to both of them now, though, and while they have the urge to let each other in on what the other one knows, they sense somehow that this is not necessary. Besides, they both know that the other one is faithful, beyond words, and so no words are necessary now, or ever in the future regarding this particular subject. A subject that needs urgent attention though is Alex's body. He is shaking, and it feels good, but it is not the kind of good that he needs to be feeling at his age.

Sabrina checks the door again, to make sure that it is locked, just because. Then she helps her man out of his shorts. The size of Alex makes it difficult for her to move him without his help, but he is very much involved in this movement, and soon enough he is lying across the center of the bed. He could be involved in what is about to happen. He could be really involved. But Sabrina decides that she will take the reins, this time, just to be on the safe side. He seems to have lost a bit of his signature self-control.

She runs her fingers up and down his shaft, which softens and then hardens, and then softens again. She really doesn't want to know what is going on inside his head and body right now, but she will definitely help him through it. She starts to finger his balls for a moment and then she squeezes them rather hard. Alex likes this a lot. She works on his balls for a moment before returning to his shaft, giving him an intricate hand job, one that certainly rivals the amateur one he received outside.

When she takes to his cock with her mouth he just closes his eyes. He knows that she's got this, completely, and so he just lets his mind drift into that mindless rushing state, as the ecstasy works itself out of his body. He doesn't even realize that she is straddling him now, riding him gently to one orgasm after the other, the drug in his system having an effect on him not unlike Viagra. Not once does he open his eyes either, trusting his wife with himself, and knowing that whatever she does to him will be for their mutual benefit.

Out on the deck Tom is livid. He pulls Mia to him, angry with himself and with her, although he isn't sure why. She did everything that he asked her to do, and it just didn't work out. Well, he must get his money's worth, and so he pulls her down with him on the chaise. Greg and Fred are already fucking the women that are with them, right there on the deck. They seem to exchange them too, passing them between themselves like coats, trying this one, and then after a moment, trying the other one.

Tom isn't in the mood for this swinging, but he is in the mood to fuck. His cock has been throbbing since he left Sabrina with Alex in the room. Shit, he was so close, he fools himself into thinking, so close to sealing the deal with the lovely Sabrina. He hadn't counted on Alex having as much self-control, as much restraint as he has clearly developed with, and because of, his new wife. Fuck it, he thinks, as he starts to finger Mia, finding her cunt warm, but not as inviting as he had already started to imagine Sabrina's would be. She will have to do, though because she is the only cunt available to him on this yacht.

He digs deep into her, trying to find something that he knows is not there. Two, then three fingers search her, her face questioning this invasion. Mia is a professional, though, and she knows it. She knows how to give a man what he wants, what he needs. She lets him finger her hard, moaning seductive, albeit rehearsed moans, and then she sighs. Mia starts to kiss his ears as he keeps fingering her, trying, she thinks, to bring her to an orgasm. Now she could fake it, but where would the fun be in that. She decides to just enjoy the fingers creeping inside her now, as the tentacles of a massive octopus.

Mia forgets where they are for the moment, the sun setting over the horizon as the yacht sails on, no particular direction, and she settles her man for the night. He is familiar to her of course, having fucked him several times during her interview, and so she almost knows what to expect. Tom takes a different turn, though, and once he has fingered her pussy wet, he turns her over and bends her down on the chaise. She thinks that he will take her pussy from the back, but instead he goes straight for her tight, sealed asshole, without lubrication, without any preparation. She lets out a loud scream.

Tom pulls her back on his cock as it

slides all the way inside her tightness, and he starts thrusting almost immediately. She is still trying to figure out what is going on her, and he is already in it for the long haul. He looks down at where his cock is disappearing into her, and he pulls and pushes her on his meat over and over again. Deeper and deeper he thrusts into her, really fucking her, really making her feel like he is the only man on her, in her. He seems to be in a whole other frame of mind now too, and Mia isn't sure what to make of it. She remembers the hefty paycheck though that she got for this trip and so if this is how he wants to fuck her then so be it.

He fucks her harder and harder, and she starts to wish he will just cum already. He doesn't though, seeming to get a second wind in the middle of the session, and he lifts her leg onto the chair, holding her thigh in his hand as he continues to move in and out of her. Then he suddenly removes his cock completely. But no sooner has he left her asshole he is back inside it. He pulls his dick all the way out again, and then quickly reinserts his thickness into the black hole that has finally relented, receiving him easier now. It is actually becoming quite nice, she thinks, at last, and so she joins the party, moving her ass around and around as he goes in and out.

Tom takes a hold of both Mia's hips now, thrusting fully into her. He is close, and he cannot hold himself back from cumming a moment longer. He looks up, closes his eyes, and shoots a massive load into her ass. Then he stirs this deposit around a little before he moves out of her. She turns to him and sucks his cock immediately. He is still cumming down, so he doesn't know what to do with her, holding her head back and off his cock for a moment just so that he can catch himself. Once he has, though, he pulls her mouth onto his softening cock and watches her suck enthusiastically on his meat, urging him towards another erection. It doesn't seem like it is going to be possible for a moment, but then he does it, getting hard unexpectedly.

He sends this new erection into her cunt, and she is now very happy. He fucks her pussy hard, and he fucks her pussy raw. There is not a trace of the man who interviewed her, the timid, unsure man who seemed a little out of his depth. This man, this Tom appears to know exactly what he wants, and he seems determined to take it. She can't help but think that if she met him under different circumstances, she might have actually liked him. There is no time for moments of nostalgic reverie, though because Tom is really going to work on her cunt. She holds herself up on the chaise, and feeds herself to him, unable to do much else.

Just before she can cum, though, he pulls his cock out of her. Then he turns her around and brings her mouth on it. She knows why. It is because he is close too and he isn't wearing a condom. Fuck, she thinks, if only he had put one on, he might have brought her to a spectacular orgasm. Now she is going to bring him to another one with her mouth, leaving her poor pussy neglected.

She starts to finger herself deep in her cunt as Tom now fucks her mouth. It isn't the way she would have liked this to end, but beggars really can't be choosers in this situation. Tom sprays his second load into her mouth, and as she swallows it, she too cums, three of her own fingers ripping into her own pussy. She shudders, and then collapses onto the chaise, reclining now, still touching herself. She is satisfied, but she is also not. She looks over to where the others are still going at it, and she suddenly wants in on that action.

Leaving Tom to pour himself a drink and go to his cabin, she joins the others. Greg and Fred are still fucking their respective whores, and the chances of getting them off are slim to none. Mia leans behind Greg and starts to lick his balls as he continues his work on the woman's cunt. He licks the balls every time he raises his ass, and then when it seems like he has figured out what is going on, he lingers longer outside the woman. Greg really loves having his balls licked.

When he brings his whore to a climax, he pulls out of her and turns to Mia, giving her better access to his nut sack now. He is still hard, still yet to cum, and so he is locked and loaded. Unlike Tom they seem to have condoms on hand, because as Mia licks his balls he changes his condom, just because of something he read somewhere some time ago. Mia does excellent work on his sack too, so much so that he feels the need to reward her. He does, and himself, by finding her pussy now with his thick, albeit short, hard cock.

Greg fucks like he speaks, rapidly. Mia has to take a moment to catch herself, to gather herself to the moment, shaking so fast under this man that she feels like she is having an epileptic fit. When she does adjust to his style, though, he is taking her pussy on a very scenic tour, meandering around the garden path and then pulling up all the roses. It is intense and feels like fireworks are going off inside her. Strangely, she likes it. She likes it so much that she is not even aware when she cums.

He keeps on going, though, fucking faster and faster. She wants to push him off her, but she knows that the nice thing to do would be to let him cum. She holds onto his neck, then onto his back, and then places her hands on his head. Her pussy has started to hurt now, though, a deep burning ache from the furious fucking she has put it through at the hands of Greg. Just a moment longer, she tells herself, he cannot possibly last much longer.

Greg does, though, and he fucks her fast and furious for a further half an hour before he finally blows. She would have had buyer's remorse too if she hadn't had two more orgasms. When he lifts off and out of her, she cannot move. Her cunt hurts really badly. She looks at the other women who seem to know what she just had to go through, and they laugh at her, helping her up and down to one of the empty cabins. They all need to shower before they rejoin the men on deck for a late dinner.

Nothing on this cruise turned out as planned, especially not for Tom. All he seems to have succeeded in doing is to bring Alex and Sabrina even closer. He tells his friends what his plan was when he invited the two of them on this joy ride, and they laugh at him. He comes clean about the ecstasy too, and Greg looks at him with a disapproving smile. They know deep down that they haven't behaved when it comes to Sabrina, and they really don't even know why themselves. They refuse to admit though that they are on the wrong side of middle-age, and it is starting to hurt.

How has Alex got it so right, though, they muse? They need to really start drinking whatever he drinks because it has apparently worked for him. He has a beautiful wife, who isn't just a trophy, and who clearly loves him for more than just his money. They think of their own lives, and how they have to hire whores or college students to entertain them because their own wives are less than satisfactory. It is not an altogether sad existence, but still, there must be more to life than this, surely.

Before they start drunk confessions of how fucked up they are and how poorly they've behaved towards their friend and his new wife, the three women return. Mia seems to have recovered, but she plays it safe this time and hangs on Tom. Greg is a little too much for her to handle. Maybe after a lot more alcohol, though, which is what Fred seems determined to do, filling everyone's glass and toasting to nothing in particular. There are worse ways to spend a weekend, and this will definitely go down as one of their favorites, sans the epiphanies of course.

Alex and Sabrina are relaxing in their room, post sex. They are not sure what to make of this whole situation, but one thing is a relief, that they can laugh at it. They do, and Alex pours them a glass of champagne. They sit in the dimly lit space and think about what has happened here, and before. They have vastly different memories of the same events but nevertheless, come to the same conclusions. They remember some events in isolation obviously, but still, they are brought back to the same place by these memories.

What is clear is that Alex's friends are total dicks. They are cunning and manipulative, and they would do anything to destroy any chance of happiness that Alex has, just for fun apparently. Yes, Sabrina is an attractive woman, but the truth is, they only want her, really want her because she belongs to Alex. There are plenty of women who are more attractive, sexier, more available than she is, so this is the only logical conclusion that any thinking adult would come to. They need to be taught a lesson, Sabrina thinks. Alex is having the same thought. They are still taken aback by the events on the yacht, though, and so the laugh again, raising their glasses to each other.

15

That was an incredible rollercoaster, and Sabrina and Alex can both not believe that they have just been a part of such a sinister plot. They look at each other, and they both just shake their heads, the words are not coming to their mouths now, so they sit silently, looking at each other. Sabrina cannot believe that she did not trust Alex, but she is grateful that she did not expose her distrust. Alex, on the other hand, is relieved that he has nothing to worry about, also relieved that his test has not been exposed.

As the yacht makes its way into the harbor, they sit and discuss a new honeymoon, one where they will not be disturbed by anyone. They actually whisper possible locations to each other now, even though the door to their cabin is locked. Then they settle on a location, a small village in Italy, somewhere that nobody would ever expect them to go. They kiss their approval of this location into one another's mouths, and then Alex has a mischievous look on his face. He asks her a question with his eyes alone, and then gets up and unlocks the door. He opens it a little, not too much, but enough for anyone who passes to have a clear view of the bed.

Sabrina seems to read his mind. If these men were willing to go to such lengths to get Sabrina into their beds, then they are going to get a show. They are going to get to see just what it is they are missing out on, what it is that they will never ever have. Alex takes his shorts off, and then his t-shirt. Sabrina throws her sarong on the floor, and then works her bikini down to the floor, passed her ankles. She pulls off the top too and then goes over to her husband on the bed.

They are not sure if anybody will pass by the room, or if they will stop and look. But they looked before, in the Caymans, and they have stolen looks at Sabrina for the longest time too. There is no reason for them not to look now. So they start to put on a very elaborate, very loud show. The sound effects are what will draw the crowd, they think correctly, and Sabrina moans loudly as she starts to suck on Alex's exaggerated penis. Alex moans loudly too, meaning it, despite the obvious need for the performance.

She holds his dick in both hands and works on his huge head. She kisses it and then bites into it, drawing louder moans from Alex. They hear someone coming down the hall, and then they hear another someone. Showtime, they think, and Sabrina starts to push his cock into her mouth, with him looking down, watching his python disappear into her beautifully perfect mouth. She sucks on it sweetly, deliciously, and she closes her eyes, really enjoying this. She even forgets the possible audience that they will have in just a moment.

Alex turns slightly so that he is not looking at the door directly. He hears, though; some movement near the door, and he knows that the morons are probably looking at them right now. Good, he thinks. He really isn't a vindictive person, and he seldom has agendas except in business. But this is one lesson that he is actually going to enjoy teaching these *sonsofbitches* that have been making his wife's life a living hell. He caresses her face as she works on his hard cock now, and he holds the base, almost milking it into her mouth now, just as a sign to show them that his is definitely bigger than theirs.

The three men scramble for positions at the door now, trying not to be seen but ensuring that they get the best view. They finally settle into their various places, Tom holding the door handle towards him, so that if Alex or Sabrina looked up, that he will be able to pull it to himself and hide their nosy faces. Alex and Sabrina know of course that they are being watched, and this was their plan anyway. So they start to really put on a show, one that none of the men outside the cabin will forget in a hurry.

Alex lifts Sabrina off the floor now, and she reluctantly lets his cock slip out of her mouth. Then he goes to his knees and parts her pussy lips with two of his fingers. He positions her in such a way that the can see everything that he is doing to her, knowing that they have seen his wife naked before, and knowing that now, he doesn't have to ever worry about them touching her. She is his, and while they can look, and while he doesn't mind them looking, he knows that they will never ever taste this beautiful blackberry that is all his.

She also doesn't mind them looking, doesn't mind them seeing her in this position. She knows that they will never own her, or taste her because she belongs entirely to the man who is now sending his tongue deep into her pussy. Alex holds her onto the floor, holding his woman in place, to stop her from falling over. He eats her cunt out with such precision that even the men watching now know, somehow, that their presence is known.

Alex works on her cunt with his tongue until she starts to cream, and he laps up every trace that is escaping her. He licks up every drop of pussy juice that is escaping from her tiny pussy, and then he nibbles on her clit again. Then he sends his tongue into her again, and licks the leftovers from the walls of her cunt, only to find his face soaked in more and more of her liquid. Sabrina stumbles now, and he is caught off-guard. He holds her up tighter, and then licks up the remainder from off of her, from inside her.

Then he stands up and lifts her off the floor completely. He carries her to the bed and places her gently down on it. Without looking at the door, he positions them so that the view is not obstructed. Then he kisses her mouth passionately, and deeply, and holds her close to him so that her cunt is in direct contact with his dick. She grinds against him, and his cock almost leans towards her, wanting inside her now more than anything.

They kiss long, and both of them forget about the audience completely now. Alex works her down onto the bed, and their lips don't part for a moment. He holds himself back from entering her, though, even though it takes everything inside him. He really just wants to take her, completely. But that will serve no purpose except to give the fuckers at the door something to jerk off too later. He needs them to see that he really loves her and that he is an expert at making love to her. He moves his lips off hers at last and goes for her neck.

He reaches her tits and takes them one at a time into his mouth. He sucks on them and really enjoys it. He throws his eyes to the door and catches their eyes on Sabrina. They are not looking at him, not really, just watching Sabrina's responses to everything that he is doing. He doesn't mind this, not at all, because he is sure that he is going to be able to draw more intense responses from her before the show is over. As he sucks on her tits, he sends a finger into her, and then another one. When he has three fingers inside her, he presses down on her clit with his thumb. She really likes this, and he knows it.

Alex continues on her tits with his mouth as he works precisely on her pussy with his fingers. The skill that this man has is incredible, way beyond his years even with the age gap. This gap doesn't even matter to Sabrina anymore; it never has actually. He really satisfies her in every way possible. He always manages to make their lovemaking new and fresh and intriguing. She bites into the top of his head, through his hair, into his scalp, as he brings her to another orgasm.

He doesn't pull his fingers from her as he goes for her mouth with his again. Alex finds her pussy deliciously warm and wet now, and so he keeps on fingering her. He has no intention of bringing her to another orgasm just yet, but that is exactly what seems like it is about to happen. There is no turning back now, though, and as he digs deeper into her, he notices that she is cumming again. He smiles to himself, knowing that he has really got her warm and ready now, and if he is going to fuck her, now would be the best time for him to get into her.

Alex positions his cock between her pussy lips and makes his way inside his wife. He is still kissing her, and then he lifts his lips off her, just to tell her that he loves her. She says she loves him too as he fills her up with his meat, and when he has gone as deep, as far as his cock could possibly go, they lock lips again. The men watching can see only Alex's ass moving up and down as he digs his cock into her. They wish that they can see more of the action that is happening on her pussy, but this is just not possible.

All three of them hold onto their dicks now, rubbing them through their shorts. They really want to take their meat out now, as it strains against the rough fabric of their shorts. But this is just not on the cards right now, since they realize that this will not look good if Alex decided to turn towards the door. They rub their heads, pre-cum already trickling out of their tools, staining their shorts in large puddles. Through this stickiness, though, they still rub their tips, knowing that this is all the action that they will see, not if they want to watch this scene play out to the end.

Alex's ass rises higher and higher, and he sinks his cock deeper into Sabrina, pulling very erotic moans from her. She is almost screaming, not so much for the performance anymore, but because her husband is really hitting the back of her pussy hard. Alex too grunts, deep guttural grunts, and the men observing this almost want to clear their throats, anything to distract them from these sounds that can only be described as primal. Remembering where they are, though, and what they are doing, they keep their own sounds to themselves.

Sabrina cums again, and then Alex, and he still thrusts into her a while longer. Then he lifts his ass high, removing his cock from her, and rolls onto his back. His dick is still solid, not that this is unusual or not to be expected, but Sabrina is still very impressed. She too has caught the audience in the corner of her eyes, and so she turns over and takes Alex's cock into her mouth, licking herself off him. This is one of her favorite parts of fucking Alex now, and she licks and laps up ever trace of their fused juices.

Then she goes for his balls, nibbling on the beach balls. She lifts them up so that the men can see that he has an impressive nut sack. She does this more for her benefit, a fuck you have a nice day to these men who have obviously seen Alex naked many times at the gym or in the locker rooms at the country club. She keeps nibbling on his huge nuts and then licks the entire surface of the sack. Sabrina runs her fingers up and down his shaft now, while she continues working on his balls. He closes his eyes, enjoying this attention immensely.

She bites into his shaft too now, digging her teeth into the not-so-sensitive flesh of her man's tool. She works up to his head again, and again, for the umpteenth time makes a valiant effort to get most of it into her mouth. She succeeds, and when he settles in the back of her throat, his moan is so loud that it borders on a scream. Someone stumbles near the door and then there is dead silence. Alex and Sabrina almost laugh out loud at this, knowing what must be going on. They don't though and return their focus to one another.

Sabrina then does something that even takes Alex by surprise. She turns to face the door and then turns away from it slightly. She positions herself on the bed now, coming up on all fours, and raises her ass towards him. He isn't sure at first if she is suggesting what he hopes she is, but then she parts her ass-cheeks with just one hand, revealing her dark, delectable rosebud. She sends a finger into it and then pulls it out very slowly. Alex looks around the room for anything that could serve as a lubricant for this succulent hole that he doesn't get to taste very often.

There is nothing on hand that can serve this purpose, and Alex starts to panic. She usually never offers him her asshole, because the last few times he had it, it was really hard for her, despite how much she tried to make him believe that it was okay. He goes up to her, and sends one of his own fingers into the tight hole, encountering immediate resistance. He pushes on, though, fingering her asshole with just this one finger, his longest one at that. He will get in her tonight if it is the last thing that he does.

As soon as her ass is receiving this one finger easily, he adds a second one. As slowly, he starts to finger her hole with just these two. Soon enough he has made progress, and her ass is receiving these two fingers easily. Still he continues to finger her with just these two, really in no hurry, and really needing to make sure that she is comfortable. She is because each time he pushes the two fingers into her she lets out such sensual sounds that he thinks that she might just be ready for a third finger to join the party.

He takes the fingers out of her asshole and puts them in his own mouth, coating three of them with a lot of spit. He doesn't want to drop wads of saliva on her asshole, thinking that this was somehow beneath her. And she is giving him an incredible gift, one which he has every intention of appreciating. He goes into her with one wet finger, and then quickly adds another. Then he starts to introduce the third finger very slowly, seeing clearly the stretch that this is resulting in. When her asshole finally starts to receive the third finger too, he is really very relieved.

Alex settles down on his heels now, kneeling behind her but literally sitting on his heels. He has to get comfortable because this is the final stretch before he tries to replace his fingers with his cock which is now set to burst with anticipation of what is coming. He pulls on it a bit with his free hand, just to placate the raging warrior, and then returns his focus to the three-finger fucking of his wife's beautiful asshole. All the way in, and then almost all the way out. All the way in, and the all the way out, he watches as her asshole snaps shut tight again in the absence of his fingers. Then he goes for it again, making an entry with all three fingers, and proceeds to finger her again.

He comes up on his heels now and rubs the tip of his cock against the side of her asshole, and against her cheeks. He pushes it against the side of her hole again and then removes just one finger. Still he teases her with the tip of his cock as he removes another finger still. When he has removed all three fingers, he has his dick aimed directly at her delicate circle. He pushes into it hard and then stops just as soon as his head has disappeared into her. Phase one of the Sabrina ass-fuck is complete.

Alex lets her adjust to his dome for a minute. He listens to her breathing, listening for anything that will let him know that the pain is unbearable. He hears nothing. He knows though that he is indeed being given access to no man's land tonight, so he is going to take his time. Fortunately, his erection doesn't seem to have any intention of going anywhere. Nowhere that is except all the way up Sabrina's delicious bubble-butt. He massages her ass cheeks now, still not moving his cock at all. If he is lucky, then she will feed herself his lengthy tool.

He parts her cheeks repeatedly, digging his fingers into them, almost pummeling them into submission. She responds by pushing against his cock, the tip tucked safely inside her, so that she starts to take his shaft into her. Every millimeter that disappears into her is an achievement, and he starts to run his fingers up and down the length of her back now too. She is going to obviously try and feed herself this tool, and he has the patience of a saint, watching himself disappear all the more into her. When they have reached halfway, she stops, and then moves herself off of his meat until just the tip is tucked into her again.

Now he starts to thrust, gently, pulling her back to him as he pushes just the half of his cock into her that has been allowed entry. He fucks her for the longest time with just this half before he tries for a little more. Two-thirds of his cock is eventually moving inside her, and he knows that he is home. There is no more necessary, and he keeps on fucking her with just this amount of cock until he has a beautiful orgasm. Then he slowly removes his cock from her and follows her down to the bed.

They lie there, loving each other, no longer concerned about the men at the door. They start to talk easily about everything but their upcoming honeymoon, and the onlookers decide that maybe it is time to move on. They walk down the hall to their own cabins, sill rock-hard, and with every intention of sorting themselves out. The women that they brought on this trip, not their wives, will have to do. Although they know that who they really want is down the hall under another man.

Alex finally gets up and closes the door, locking it. Sabrina looks impressed with herself, and Alex too, and they laugh at this evening's events. They must be close to the harbor now, so that they shower together, washing each other off each other, and then making love again. The shower is small, but it is not too small that they both don't fit in it. They discuss their honeymoon now, alone, with the safety of the running water. When they are in bed again, relaxing and drinking champagne, they burst into laughter. They are not sure how it got to this, and how the men down the hall could have underestimated their love for each other. One thing is certain, though, there will be no such underestimations in the near future, or in fact, ever again.

AUTHOR'S NOTE

Readers: I want to expand a few of the stories to see where the characters can be explored further. If there are any of the stories that you would like to read more about again, I'd love to hear from you!

Visit my blog at http://www.jaelynnmccranie.com/

Join my newsletter for free exclusive previews
http://jaelynnmccranie.com/newsletter/

Follow me on Twitter at
http://www.twitter.com/jaelynnmccranie

Like my page on Facebook at
https://www.facebook.com/jaelynnmccranieauthor

Discover my books at major ebook retailers everywhere.